finding
day's
bottom

finding
day's
bottom

CANDICE RANSOM

 CAROLRHODA BOOKS, INC. MINNEAPOLIS NEW YORK

Carolrhoda Books, Inc.
A division of Lerner Publishing Group
241 First Avenue North
Minneapolis, MN 55401 U.S.A.

Website address: www.lernerbooks.com

Library of Congress Cataloging-in-Publication Data

Ransom, Candice F., 1952–
 Finding Day's Bottom / by Candice Ransom.
  p. cm.
 Summary: After her father dies, eleven-year-old Jane-Ery slowly finds
healing through her relationship with her grandfather and their rural
Virginia home.
 ISBN-13: 978–1–57505–933–4 (lib. bdg. : alk. paper)
 ISBN-10: 1–57505–933–9 (lib. bdg. : alk. paper)
 [1. Grief—Fiction. 2. Fathers and daughters—Fiction. 3. Grandfathers—
Fiction. 4. Country life—Virginia—Fiction. 5. Virginia—History—20th
century—Fiction.] I. Title.
PZ7.R1743Fe 2006
[Fic]—dc22   2005033369

Manufactured in the United States of America
1 2 3 4 5 6 – BP – 11 10 09 08 07 06

To my husband, Frank,
who has always protected me

contents

grandpap

The spring my daddy died, Grandpap came down from Salter's Mountain to live with Mama and me.

"I'm glad to get out," he said. "My place was so far back in the hills, the hoot owl hollered at noon."

"So? I've heard owls hoot in the daytime," I said. Grandpap studied me a minute, then went out to unload his pickup.

"Why is Grandpap here now?" I asked Mama.

"It's not good for old people to stay by themselves," Mama said. "He needs us."

"Grandpap can't take Daddy's place," I said. "He'd

better not even try."

Grandpap moved into my little room behind the kitchen. I put my things in Mama's room. Since Daddy died, I'd been sleeping in the big feather bed that was hers and Daddy's anyway. Mama gave me her pillow. At night she laid her head on Daddy's pillow with a long sigh.

Mama didn't cry much. Mostly she stayed awake, staring up at the ceiling. She picked at her finger-nails, making a clicking sound. I figured she was fret-ting about how we'd get by without Daddy's pay from the sawmill.

This morning before I cracked my eyelids, I put my hand across my stomach. After a whole month, my insides still had that scooped-out feeling. I didn't want to see this room or house or yard ever again. Not without my father in it.

The last time I saw Daddy, he said, "See you tonight, Miss Mousie." That's what he called me, from when I was little.

He always sang "Froggie Went a-Courtin'" on his way home. I'd run out to meet him as he sang real loud, "Miss Mousie, won't you marry me?"

"Yes!" I'd say, and he'd swing me around, even after I got too big.

I was in school later that morning when the sawmill whistle blew six shrill blasts. The somebody's-been-hurt signal.

With that sound echoing in my head, I opened my eyes. Nobody would ever call me Miss Mousie again. Nobody would sing me silly songs. I crawled into the day, hollow and slow.

The smell of fried grits and red-eye gravy drifted from the kitchen. After Grandpap came, Mama fixed us real breakfasts again. Side meat and corncakes. Or sausage and white gravy over biscuits. I'd gotten fair tired of cornmeal mush and sorghum.

Grandpap rolled out of bed first to toss pine knots into the woodstove's firebox.

"Old bones shouldn't lay long," he said. "Or they

get stiff."

He parched green coffee beans on the stove, stirring them till they turned brown, then ground them in the hand-cranked coffee mill. Sometimes I put my treasures in the little wooden drawer of the coffee mill. Four-leaf clovers, the first bird's-foot violet of May.

Once I hid a smooth round stone in the drawer. Daddy ground it with the coffee beans. He was hopping mad! But not for long. Daddy never stayed mad at me for long.

That day he told me where coffee came from. Not Parson's Store, where we bought beans in a cloth sack, but far-off Araby, a country where men wore long robes and rode bumpety camels across the desert.

"Have you ever been to Araby?" I asked him.

"No," Daddy said. "Furthest I've been is Richmond-city."

"I wisht I could go to the city," I said. I'd never been out of the mountains.

"I'll take you," Daddy had promised. "On your

birthday."

But he never kept that promise. I turned eleven a week after his funeral.

"Can I have some coffee?" I asked now, sliding into my seat. Grandpap's coffee put me in mind of Daddy. I wondered what far-off Araby tasted like.

"You know I don't hold with children drinking coffee," Mama said.

"I'm old enough to take over some of Daddy's chores."

Mama gave me a look. "Jane-Ery," was all she had to say. She set my usual glass of buttermilk in front of me.

"Let her have a little, Paulett," said Grandpap. "Won't hurt." Grandpap was Mama's father. He could sweet-talk her into just about anything.

"A *little*," Mama agreed. She pulled an envelope from her apron pocket and shoved it under the sugar bowl.

The blue and white sugar bowl with one cracked handle belonged to my grandmother. Mama's mama.

Grandpap's wife. It had sat on our kitchen table since the day Granny died, three years before I was born. Mama once told me that the sugar bowl held more memories of her mother than all the picture albums in the world.

The tail of the envelope peeked out from beneath the sugar bowl. Red letters were stamped across one end, but I couldn't read them.

Grandpap poured me half a cup of coffee from the blue-speckled coffeepot.

"Best way to start the day," he said, drinking deeply from his own cup. "I like mine barefooted."

"What?" Grandpap said the strangest things.

"Without milk and sweetenin'."

I sipped, then choked, spraying coffee all over the red-checked oilcloth. My eyes blurred from the bitter taste.

Mama wiped the mess with a rag. "I told you you're too young."

"Let's do this." Grandpap took the saucer from beneath my cup. He poured milk in the saucer, stirred in a teaspoon of white table sugar, then added a splash of coffee.

"That doesn't look like real coffee," I said.

"Try it," said Grandpap.

I did. His concoction was good!

"You just like your'n with socks on," he said. "I'll have a dram more."

Daddy always liked me to pour his coffee. Without thinking I reached for the metal handle of the pot the same time Grandpap did. Our fingers touched, his knobbly and work-hardened, mine long and thin.

"Will you do the honors?" he said.

I poured, careful not to spill a drop.

"Ahhh," Grandpap said, setting his cup down with a clink. "Sufficient unto the day is the evil thereof."

"What does *that* mean?"

"I have no idea. But it sounds grand, don't it?"

The sun peeked through Mama's feed sack curtains. The same sun that shone over Araby. And

Richmond-city. Soft light lay over the kitchen like the grace Daddy used to say at meals.

I sipped my dish of coffee-milk. Warmth spread through my insides, seeping into the sharp corners. For the first time in many weeks, I didn't feel hollow.

Mama sank into the chair opposite me. She ate two bites of fried grits, then laid her fork down.

"You don't eat enough to keep a jaybird alive," Grandpap told her.

"Buddy came back from the war overseas without a scratch," Mama said, staring into space, "and gets kilt right here at home. I keep thinkin' if only I'd put two sandwiches in his dinner bucket that day. He would have taken longer to eat 'em. Instead, he ate fast and was back on the job just in time for that truck . . ." She broke off and said faintly, "He needed a haircut."

Mama talked about Daddy like that sometimes, out of the blue. Then his name wouldn't pass her lips for days.

I started to touch her sleeve, but Mama pushed her plate away.

She looked at me then, as if she remembered who I was. "Chore time, Missy. How long you goin' to keep those hens waitin'?"

My chair made a harsh scraping sound as I got up.

ramp supper

"Jane-Ery," Mama said a few mornings later. "Can't you sit still?"

"She's got the jim-jams," Grandpap said. "It's spring."

My feet had the fidgets, all right. "Can I go outside?"

"Done your chores yet?" she asked.

"Can't I do them a little later?"

"What if I let the chores go?" Mama said. "What if I stopped washin' the clothes and scrubbin' the floor and choppin' kindlin? Wouldn't we be in a fix?"

When Daddy was alive, he'd sometimes tell me to

run along, and he'd feed the hogs. And if Mama lit into me for loafing or daydreaming, sometimes he'd take up for me. But nobody stood between me and Mama now.

"I didn't say I wasn't *going* to do them. Just not this second." Mama and I looked at each other across the table.

Finally Grandpap said, "Jane-Ery, you're your mama made all over again. Even if you do have your daddy's mama's name." He grinned. "Jane-Footy."

Now I stared at him. "What?"

"Don't you memorize? I used to call you Jane-Footy. You were barely out of hippin's but you'd squench up them brown eyes and say, plain as day, 'My name is Jane-*Ee-ry.*'"

He cackled and Mama clapped the lid on the sugarbowl in embarrassment.

"Heaven's sake, Pap. Nobody says 'hippins' anymore. It's *diapers.*"

"I'm just sayin' Jane-Ery's got a point." Grandpap

scraped his thumbnail with his case knife. "Seems to me you weren't too broke out in work yourself when you were her age."

Red blotches rose on Mama's neck. "I worked hard, Pap. You don't remember because you were away in the logging camp."

My stomach was starting to hurt. I didn't want to be the cause of any more arguing.

"Can I go out after I do my work?" I asked.

The deep crease between Mama's eyes smoothed a little. "Run on, then. Get some greens for tonight's supper."

"A ramp supper!" Grandpap grinned in delight. "Nothin' says spring like ramps. Are we havin' pinto beans and griddle cakes, too?"

"I reckon," said Mama.

The hens didn't have time to settle their feathers before I snatched their eggs and left. Then I slopped the hogs. Next I fed the geese, dodging the mean one that liked to nip my ankles.

Last, I milked Clover. Daddy used to sing "Chinquapin Pie" when he milked. Said it relaxed the cow. Daddy had a fine singing voice, but I wasn't the least little bit tuneful. Clover might kick if I sang.

After taking the milk in to Mama, I flew out the door again.

"Want some company?" Grandpap asked from the porch.

I didn't want Grandpap slowing me down. But I said, "Sure."

"I know where ramps grow thick," he said. "Right up this walk-path."

We walked up the trail. Contrary Creek followed alongside, talking to us the whole way. Spring beauties bloomed beneath a witch's hobble. The tree was putting out tiny leaves.

Spring moved slow in the mountains. Winter, with its grays and browns and rags of snow, hung on like an old hurt.

Daddy showed me how color crept in, a green so

new, it was still yellow along the edges. A green that could heal. He taught me to pay attention before dark-green laurel, honeysuckle, and wisteria chased the gold away.

On a sunny ridge, wild garlic waved their long tops in the breeze. Near the creek bank, Grandpap scuffed dead leaves with the toe of his boot, revealing several plants with broad leaves.

"What'd I tell you?" he said cheerfully. "This scoundrel mountain is *thick* with ramps."

"Phew!" I pinched my nose shut. "Stinks like rotten eggs!"

"Ain't you ever had ramps before?"

I shook my head. "Daddy wasn't too keen over them."

"Ramps is larripin' good," Grandpap said. "You don't know what you're missin'."

We dug ramps, filling our basket.

Grandpap rinsed a couple in the creek and gave me one.

"Try it," he said. "It'll put hair on your chest."

"I'm a girl! I don't want hair on my chest."

I didn't want the onion either, after I'd had one bite. "It tastes like it smells."

Grandpap laughed at my face. "Schoolteacher used to tell us young'uns don't come to school after eatin' ramps. Course I did, so I'd get sent home."

Next we gathered dandelion leaves, brook lettuce, and something Grandpap called turkey mustard.

He rested a spell while I wandered. I picked purple and white confederate violets. A bluebird sang in a laurel bush, pretty as any calendar picture. I tried to whistle his song. My spirits lifted a bit.

I climbed to the top of the ridge and looked down. Away and beyond were miles and miles of trees, rocks, vines, bushes.

Daddy's sight was keener than a hawk's in December. Once he gazed across the valley and said, "Yonder's a bear's den."

"Where? I don't see it," I'd said, jumping all around.

He gently turned my head a bit. "See that snaggle-tooth pine? Now look to the left. Don't stare right at it front-ways. Kind of glance at it side-like."

At last the confusion of branches sorted itself and I spied the gap in the rock.

But I never would have guessed it was there. Daddy had a way of making sense of the woods. I always thought trees just grew and birds just flew around and rocks just sat in the path. But Daddy said everything was on this earth for a reason.

I looked for the den now, hoping to see a mama bear with cubs. But sunshine and shadow played tag. My eyes couldn't catch hold of any one thing.

I turned and walked down the ridge. The bluebird was gone.

"Ready to head back?" Grandpap asked.

"Yes," I said, sensing the greeny-gold woods had already grown a shade darker. "Let's go."

Back home, Mama had a new chore lined up. All

of us picked up sticks in the garden. Fall and winter, the wind blew branches and twigs in our garden plot. We couldn't plow until the ground was clear.

All that stooping and picking, stooping and picking made me tired. My legs felt like poplar logs. I sat down on a thin patch of grass.

"I don't have a spoonful of ambition," I said. I thought Mama would yell at me for laziness.

Instead she said, "That's the way of it this time of year. You have to build up to outside work. Grandpap and I'll finish. Go in and get dinner started."

I fixed egg salad sandwiches on soft, white bread Mama had bought at Parson's Store as a treat. We didn't have light bread too much. We didn't go to Parson's Store much, neither.

When I used to go with Daddy, he'd give me a nickel to buy candy, penny a pick. I'd ponder whether to get five different pieces of candy. Or blow the whole nickel on a tiny carton of Nik-L-Nip wax bottles, filled with colored syrup. But now when I go to

Parson's Store with Mama, she says we don't have an extra nickel to waste on foolishness.

Next I set the table. As I moved the sugar bowl, I saw the envelope Mama had tucked under it at breakfast. The stamped letters read "Past Due." No wonder Mama clicked her fingernails at night. Were there other bills she was late paying?

What would we do for money, now that Daddy was gone?

When Mama and Grandpap came in, I didn't let on I'd seen the past-due bill.

And Mama didn't let on anything was wrong. While I chopped the greens, she said, "Look at them flies. The window screen is black with 'em. Ramps draws flies, for some reason."

She poured corncake batter on the griddle, flipping the cakes once so they got crispy but not burnt. Then she heated leftover pinto beans with a little bacon grease. She drizzled the rest of the heated bacon grease over the chopped greens. Grandpap put the pitcher of buttermilk on the table and we sat down.

Daddy always gave the blessing before meals. Not the usual kind, but about little things. If he were here this evening, he might say, "Thank you, Lord, for letting us fill our souls with Your new-green trees today."

Grandpap grabbed the corncake platter and dug right in.

"How come you don't say grace?" I asked him.

"I don't hold much with talkin' to my plate," he said.

"You're supposed to be talking to the Lord."

"Jane-Ery," Mama warned.

"Daddy used to say the best ones. Not too long," I said. "He was always asked to give the blessing at church socials."

Grandpap drank a slug of buttermilk. "I don't hold much with churchfyin', neither." He spoke lightly, but with an undertone that told me to quit harping on it.

Mama wrinkled her nose as she passed the bowl of

ramps to Grandpap. "I don't know how you can eat this stuff."

He heaped his plate. "Ramps is good for your heart, did you know that?" He held the dish out to me. "Sure you don't want some, Jane-Ery?"

The grease-glistened ramps smelled so rank, there couldn't have been any healing in them. I shook my head.

"Meal fit for a king," Grandpap said, holding a piece of corncake dripping with butter. "Let the flat-landers have their T-bone steaks!"

Mama pushed her food around her plate. She kept glancing over at the envelope under the sugar bowl.

I wondered how much money we owed. Must be a powerful lot to rob Mama of her appetite.

looking for day's bottom

After supper, I stepped outside again. The sky glowed pinky-orange as the sun dipped over the ridge. Good walking time.

Grandpap followed me out on the porch.

"Where you off to, Jane-Ery?"

"Nowhere."

I didn't want to tell him about Daddy and me. But the words fell out of my mouth anyway.

"Used to, Daddy and me would ramble after supper. Take some air. My feet still feel like walking but the rest of me doesn't want to."

Grandpap sat in the hickory rocker and took a few crumbs of tobacco from his overalls pocket. He stuffed his pipe, lit a match on the sole of his boot.

"Have a set," he said.

I sat on the bucket bench next to him.

"I used to be an after-supper rambler myself," he said. "But then I got old and worn out and found the air on the porch just as fresh."

"Where'd you go?" I asked.

He puffed a long while. "Here and there. Sometimes I'd go looking for Day's Bottom."

"Day's Bottom?" I asked. "Where's that?"

"Far off yonder," Grandpap said. "A place of light and wonderment."

"But where *is* it?"

"Told you. I'm still lookin' for it."

I chewed a piece of hair and thought out loud. "Lights . . . electric lights, probably. Where would there be lots of lights?"

Grandpap just rocked and puffed, not giving up a

single hint.

Cade and Blue Creedy once told me about going to the firemen's carnival in New Market. They carried on about spinning rides and glittering lights until I wanted to go, too. Eat a cloud of pink cotton candy and get dizzy on the Ferris wheel.

"Is Day's Bottom a carnival?" I said, hoping I was right.

"Don't think it's a carnival," Grandpap said.

I thought some more. "Is it—a car race?"

Exie Dills, our neighbor down the creek, owned a radio. Some Saturday nights we'd visit. I'd lay on the floor-rug, listening to the live broadcast of stock-car races at Sumerduck Speedway. In the background, crowds yelled excited-like, while I pictured a duck-shaped car zipping around the track.

"Might be," said Grandpap, his face lost in pipesmoke. "Then again, might not."

I looked up at the sky, as if the answer might be written in the orange-tinged clouds. "It's not—

heaven, is it?"

Grandpap threw back his head and laughed.

Anger boiled up inside of me. "You're fooling me. You made up Day's Bottom, didn't you?"

"Believe what you want," he said. "You still going ramblin'?"

My feet twitched to tramp down the hog-pen path, up the hill, and over to the old log flume. Daddy and I would rest there, not talking, just taking in the peacefulness of the woods getting ready for bed.

"I don't think so." It wouldn't be the same.

Quiet stretched between Grandpap and me like a spiderweb. Grandpap didn't seem bothered by the silence. He drew on his pipe, watching the sky go from orange to red. Behind us, Mama's lamp gleamed the color of his pocket watch.

"You ever hear the story about the stingy old woman?" he asked.

I shook my head.

"Well, once there was this stingy old woman. She

only ate ashcakes and water and kept her moneybag up the chimney," he said.

I leaned forward in the gathering dark and he continued.

"The old woman's hired girl found her moneybag. She couldn't stuff the bag up the chimney again, so she buried the coins in the ashes. Then she run off, scared the old woman would be after her, madder than a dog in August.

"The hired girl met a horse with a sore back, a cow that needed milkin', and a peach tree with loaded-down branches. She rubbed the horse's back, milked the cow, and propped up the peach tree's branches."

"I thought she was in a hurry," I said.

Grandpap paid me no mind. "The old woman, she come home and found her moneybag gone. She lit out after the hired girl. Saw the horse standin' there. The horse asked would she rub his back. The old woman said no, but asked if he'd seen the thievin' hired girl.

"'Gallymanders! Gallymanders!'" Grandpap screeched in an old lady's voice that made me giggle. "'All my gold and silver's gone! My great long moneypurse!'

"The horse let on like he hadn't. The old woman went on. Saw the cow. The old woman wouldn't milk the cow, but she asks if Old Bossy has seen her hired girl. The cow said no. The old woman kept runnin'."

"Then she went to the peach tree," I said.

"Who's tellin' this story, you or me?" Grandpap puffed indignantly, then went on. "The old woman asked the peach tree where her hired girl went. The peach tree asked her to fix its branches, but the old woman said no. So the peach tree made like it hadn't seen the hired girl. The old woman went home. Last I heard, that stingy old woman was still livin' on ashcakes and water. And she hadn't found her moneypurse."

"If she fixed corncakes in the ashes, stands to reason she'd find her money," I said.

"It's a story, Jane-Ery," Grandpap said.

Funny thing about that story. It made my feet stop fidgeting.

"Can you tell me a story about Day's Bottom?" I asked.

He puffed a while. "Don't know any stories about Day's Bottom. Just things that happened to me."

"What things?"

"Well, last week I popped a shirt button," he finally said.

I wondered what that had to do with Day's Bottom.

"Your mama wanted to sew it back on, but weren't no use lookin' for it."

"Why?" I asked.

"Cause it's in Day's Bottom."

"Buttons fly clear to Day's Bottom!" My curiosity rose up like fur on a cat's back.

"Yes, indeedy."

I propped my elbows on my knees. "Is it a fine place? The finest place in the world?"

"Right now, crawling between the covers sounds like the finest place in the world." Grandpap puffed his pipe. "After pickin' up all them sticks in the garden, I'm ready for bed."

I stared at the buckled floorboards. Mama and Grandpap did my share of work earlier. "Where do you think Day's Bottom is?"

"Wisht I knew. I never could locate it."

"I bet I can."

He winked at me. "It might could take two people. How 'bout if you look high and I look low?"

"You're teasing me again!"

"No, I'm not," he said. "When should we start?"

In my mind, Day's Bottom was filled with candy and ice cream, everything free. Like Parson's Store— no! a better store, like the biggest five and ten in Virginia. With toys and games and lace-trimmed white ankle socks and one of those stuffed cloth dogs your friends write their names on, autograph hounds. *That* was Day's Bottom. Not a place of lost buttons.

Maybe the stingy old woman's great long money-purse was there, too. If it was, I'd grab a handful of silver coins and give them to Mama to pay the past due bill.

And have enough left over to get me fifty picks of penny candy at Parson's Store.

"Tomorrow," I answered Grandpap. "We'll start looking tomorrow."

parson's store

Mama had other ideas about what I was going to do.

"You can't traipse off when there's so much to be done around here. Why do you think I took you out of school?" she said when I told her I wanted to go walking.

I thought I'd got out of school early because of Daddy. I couldn't keep my mind on my studies. And the other kids acted like I was invisible all of a sudden.

Jeff Suttle, who used to be my best friend, didn't pick me for his kickball team at recess anymore, even though I was the best kicker. Nobody else could wham the ball with their instep, then run barefoot around the bases.

Just because Daddy was gone didn't mean I was, too.

"You and Pap are putting the garden in today," Mama told me after breakfast.

The night before, Grandpap had studied the farmer's almanac. He read moving his lips, I noticed. But that was okay. I counted everything in twos by running my tongue across the roof of my mouth.

"The next few days are in Pisces, a fruitful sign," he said. "And the moon is on the increase. Best time to plant crops that grow above the ground."

"You should plant potatoes in the dark of the moon," I had added, showing off. Daddy had planted by the moon and signs, too.

"Jane-Ery," Mama said now. "Wake up. Pap's waitin'. I swear, you're moony as a white horse."

Heat prickled the back of my neck as I stomped out on the porch.

Grandpap got up from the rocker. "I thought you'd gone back to bed."

"You're as bad as Mama!"

"Just teasin', Jane-Ery. You're lookin' out of heart."

"Work," I said. "It never seems to end."

Grandpap nodded. "You can hate work like a January blizzard. Or you can try to find some pleasure in it. Either way, it's got to be done."

In the garden patch, a stiff wind nearly blew us upside down. The bright sun made it feel less chilly, though.

Grandpap had borrowed Exie Dills's mule to plow our plot. Then he dragged the harrow over it. When the soil was fine as frog's hair split four ways, we marked off rows. Grandpap stuck a notched twig in the ground with one end of a string tied to it. I unrolled the string ball, putting one foot straight in front of the other, to the other side.

Grandpap walked behind his old one-foot push plow. I trailed after him, dropping bean seeds in the furrow. He came back with the plow, turning the dirt over. I tamped the dirt down with my shoe, making sure each seed was covered. Whenever we passed each other, Grandpap told me a riddle.

"Jane-Ery. Who's buried in Grant's tomb?"

He almost tripped me on that one.

Mama came out with a jug of cold water. By now Grandpap and I were sweating.

"You've both been working up a storm," she said. "Pap, can you run down to Parson's? I got something on the stove I don't want to leave."

"Let me get cleaned up first," he said. "Want to ride along, Jane-Ery?"

Did I! I hadn't been to Parson's Store in ages.

I scrubbed off the garden grime quick and climbed in Grandpap's old truck before Mama thought of something else for me to do.

Grandpap didn't drive like an old man. He mashed the gas pedal hard and that rattle-trap truck jolted all over the rutted road. I bounced around the front seat like popcorn.

Pickups and a couple rusty cars were parked in front of Parson's. We got out and went inside. The wooden door hadn't seen a lick of paint in years and the Coca-Cola sign hanging above it was sun-faded. When the door slapped behind us, everyone inside turned our way.

"Hi-dy, Willard." Rush Suttle waved his pipe at Grandpap. He and Amos Creedy were playing checkers. They used Coca-Cola caps with the game board plopped on a pickle barrel.

"Rush, Amos." Grandpap tugged the bill of his cap. "What're you two old liars up to?"

"Up to no good," Rush answered. "No good a-tall."

The men laughed.

Grandpap pulled a limp dollar from his shabby billfold. "Jane-Ery, fetch a gallon of coal oil and a sack of white flour." He handed me the gas can. "And buy something sweet for yourself."

I looked at him. "Did Mama say I could?"

"I said you could. Now run along."

Grandpap joined the checker-players. I heard them talking about Decoration Day, coming up tomorrow. Mama hadn't said a word about it. I figured we weren't going, with Daddy just gone and all.

I didn't want to go anyway. Didn't want to see Daddy's sad-looking grave without a sprig of grass. I bet Mama didn't want to either.

I bought the flour and coal oil from Burt Parson, then got myself a Black Cow sucker because it lasted the longest.

"How you farin', Miss Jane-Ery?" Amos Creedy asked.

"Fine," I mumbled.

"My boys can't wait to see you tomorry," he said. The Creedy boys were uglier than homemade mud. Cade Creedy teased me something awful in Sunday School. I wasn't tearing myself to see them.

"I don't think we're going," I said, glancing at Grandpap. He didn't nod or shake his head.

"Course you are!" Rush Suttle said. "Everyone gets together on Decoration Day to . . . " He cleared his throat. "Well, you know."

Grandpap gathered up the gas can and sack of flour. "Time we were off. See you fellas."

"We're not going tomorrow, are we?" I asked Grandpap as he loaded the supplies in the back of the pickup. "Mama hasn't said anything."

"Jane-Ery, I don't know what your mother is thinking from one minute to the next. And that's the truth of it."

On the way home, I nearly poked my eye out trying to eat the sucker, the way he drove. But I finished it and threw the stick under the porch so Mama wouldn't know.

In the kitchen, Mama had dragged out every baking pan. She took the flour from me at once.

"Jane-Ery, I need you. We're baking biscuits for Decoration Day."

"I thought we weren't going."

"What gave you that idea?"

"You never said we were."

"And I never said we weren't. When have we ever missed Decoration Day? Now hand me the can of lard."

Mama dumped flour into a clean dishpan.

"How many biscuits are we making?" I asked.

"Five hundred or so."

I blew my bangs out in a puff of air. "That's a pile of biscuits."

Mama mixed lard into the flour with her strong fingers. "I used to roll out fifty biscuits of a morning, and I was younger than you. Nowadays kids don't know the meaning of work."

Why was Mama always saying stuff like that? Could I help it I didn't have four older brothers like she did when she was growing up? Or that her mother made her wash dishes from the time she was three years old? Mama told me how she had to stand on a stool to reach the basin.

We baked all afternoon. At first I ate a couple hot out of the oven, dripping with butter. But then I got so I couldn't look at another biscuit.

That night, I laid out my best dress, green calico with a white scalloped collar. The last time I'd worn it was to Daddy's funeral. I never wanted to set foot in the burial ground again.

But I was going tomorrow, whether I wanted to or not. Mama would see to it.

decoration day

Cars and trucks were parked hood to trunk across
the road from the churchyard.

People swarmed up the hill like ants in a puddle of
molasses, toting blankets and baskets and babies.

Every year on the last day of May, people all over
Purgatory Mountain gathered at Mount Olive Free
Will Baptist Church to clean up the graves and dec-
orate them with flowers. Everyone had a big time,
catching up after a long winter.

"Hope them young'uns didn't shuck their shoes
before the tenth," Grandpap said when a gaggle of

kids ran barefoot in front of us.

"Why?" I asked, wiggling my own bare toes.

"Bad luck."

"Mama, is that true?" I'd kicked off my shoes weeks ago.

"The ground holds winter damp well into May," Mama said. "And *that's* true."

Why would Grandpap say something like that? To make me think I'd have more bad luck? How could things be any worse?

When I stepped out of Grandpap's pickup, I saw some girls from my class.

"Hi-dy," I said.

"Hi-dy," Doris Hicks mumbled. She twitched like she was still wearing her wool longjohns.

Lorraine Dickinson stared over my right shoulder. She hadn't looked me in the eye since my daddy's accident.

Both of their fathers worked at the sawmill. It could have been Doris's or Lorraine's daddy who got

kilt that day. Maybe that was what they were thinking as they walked away.

Mama handed dishtowel-covered baskets to me,
along with our oldest quilt. "Find a good spot, then
come back for more baskets."

"We shoulda brought the wheelbarrow,"
Grandpap grumbled, taking six baskets at once. "Be
easier than making forty-eleven trips."

I found a level spot under a pin oak tree and
spread the quilt. Daddy used to joke that I always
slipped rocks under the quilt when we had a dinner
on the ground.

People we hadn't seen since the funeral came over
to speak to us.

"How you getting along?" Mrs. Carter asked
Mama. Her voice was sticky as warm molasses.

"Tolerable," Mama replied. "Pap is a big help.
And Jane-Ery."

Mrs. Carter peered at me. "Well, you *ought* to be a
help to your mama. Big girl like you."

"Yes'm," I said, staring at the hairy mole on the end of her nose.

The trestle table, a door on sawhorses, was loaded down with food of all sorts. Some women from church asked Mama when we were coming back.

"Maybe next Sunday," she said.

"Did you make all these biscuits?" Blue Creedy asked me, peeking under the corner of a dishtowel.

"I helped."

He dropped the dishtowel. "Well, I ain't eatin' none."

"Suit yourself." He was just a stupid boy.

Cade Creedy elbowed his brother out of the way. "Pay him no mind, Jane-Ery. I'll eat anything you fixed."

Cade had a little crush on me. When we were learning about the apostles, Cade added "Cade the Greater" and "Blue the Lesser" just to hear me giggle. He looked hopeful, but today I didn't feel like idle talk.

Exie Dills sidled up to Mama. He'd lived alone ever since his wife had run off. He came to tend his folks' graves.

"I thought I smelled Paulett's state fair biscuits," he said. He snicked one and ate it in two bites. "Makes you want to slap your Grandma Bob!"

"Go on with you." Mama acted put out, but she gave him a ghost of a smile.

Exie nodded at me. "Good to see you both again, in happier times."

Mama busied herself arranging platters. She did not answer him.

I walked over to where Grandpap was pulling weeds on Granny's grave. I bent to brush acorn caps and pine needles from the weathered headstone.

"Sometimes I can't believe Nettie isn't still with us," Grandpap said. "I swear I can hear her yell, 'Chop wood!'" He chuckled. "I thought 'Chop Wood' was my name the longest time."

I wished I had known my grandmother. Or my

Uncle Rafe, Mama's brother who had been shot in a hunting accident when he was only sixteen. Next to Rafe was Uncle Dan. He never came back from the war against Hitler.

"'Durn infernal Hilter,' Nettie used to fume," said Grandpap. "His name ain't Hilter, I told her a hundred times. It's *Hit*ler."

I tried not to look, but it was hard to miss the mound of newly turned earth under the persimmon tree. Daddy's grave wasn't marked with a headstone. Mama hadn't paid the stonecutter yet.

Everybody sang and talked as they pulled weeds and trimmed grass and planted flowers. I could almost hear Daddy leading the singing of "Let the Circle Be Unbroken" like he did last year. Decoration Day was a day to remember those who had passed.

But I didn't want to remember. The hurt inside of me was as raw as the dirt on Daddy's grave. I looked over at the Creedys. Cade and Blue had more relatives than you could shake a stick at. Why did our circle, the smallest family on Purgatory Mountain, have to be broken?

Mama kneeled beside me. Her face was tight from trying not to cry. This day was hard on her, too.

"We shouldn't have come," I said.

"We can't stay shut up forever. Besides, nobody makes biscuits good as mine. Folks count on them." She laid a ribbon-tied posy of wildflowers on Daddy's grave.

Wake-robin was scarce as preachers in paradise, as Grandpap liked to say. Red blossoms and pale white blossoms grew from the same stem, like two different plants.

I touched dark red petals. "Where did you find them?"

"Down by the creek," Mama said. "You aren't the only person who goes ramblin', Jane-Ery."

I put my hand on the mound of earth. It still seemed hard to believe Daddy's body was under there. Or was it?

"Is Daddy in heaven with Granny and Uncle Rafe and Uncle Dan?" I asked.

"Yes, Jane-Ery."

"How'd he find them?"

"They were waiting for him," Mama said.

"But he was kilt in an accident. How'd they know he was coming?" I tugged a single blade of crabgrass that had dared to grow on Daddy's grave. The blade came out of the dirt hard, as if it believed it had a right to be there.

"His angel told his kin," she said. "That's how."

I wrestled with another thought. "Remember what Preacher Cassell said at Daddy's funeral? About all the mansions in Lord's house? And how heaven is a billion houses in the biggest house of all?"

Mama nodded. She looked uncomfortable, like she had a crick in her hip.

I yanked the thought out like the stubborn grass. "If all the people who ever died in the world are crammed up in heaven, how will I ever find Daddy? When I die, I mean."

"You just will," Mama said quietly.

I still wasn't sure I would.

Everybody was supposed to have an angel. Suppose mine forgot me, like that time in first grade I played like I was asleep at naptime? The other kids went out for recess and I had to stay in.

When they came back, laughing and trailing cold air, they seemed surprised to see me on my old rug. I sat up, blinking, the nap of the rug printed on my cheek, feeling like I'd thrown away a whole hour of my life.

Now I pictured my angel off at recess, skipping rope maybe, while I waited outside the Pearly Gates, looking for Daddy between the golden bars.

I suddenly felt tired. "Mama, can we go?"

"We haven't eaten yet."

I didn't mean the churchyard. I wanted to leave Purgatory Mountain for good, go where we wouldn't

see Daddy-shaped holes every place we looked.
I was ready to go to Day's Bottom.

job's tears

Grandpap and I hoed the garden patch every morning before it got too hot. Even then, the sun burned the back of my neck.

"This dirt is so poor, Jane-Ery," Grandpap whispered, "we can't raise nothin', not even our voice."

I giggled. Such fool-talk!

But Grandpap knew right smart about growing things. His tomato plants stood up straighter when he passed. The squash flowered proud and the bush beans grew in lush, leafy waves.

He even dabbled in yarbs. I recognized yarrow and

touch-me-not. Mama often picked both plants along the road. Yarrow leaves could stop bleeding and touch-me-not helped cure poison oak.

"This here's Job's tears." Grandpap's fingers brushed a tall grassy plant knobbed with hard round seeds. "These little seeds have a secret."

"What?"

He broke one off and slit it with his case knife. "Inside each one are three tiny flowers. They're a little garden in themselves."

"What do you do with them?" I asked.

"Some people string the seeds to help babies cut teeth. But mostly people make jewelry. See? It already has a hole in it." He dropped the seed in my palm. "They're good luck to carry around, too."

I slipped it in my pocket. "Why are they called Job's tears?"

"Job was a fella in the Bible," Grandpap said. "He had a world of troubles. Lost his money, his family. I guess his woes made him cry a lot. These seeds look like his tears."

I looked across the yard where Mama hung up sheets. The wind filled them like sails on a ship.

Mama could have been Job's sister. She didn't cry, but her shoulders were bowed. I tried to help her all I could, but sadness and worry clung to her like a wet rag.

"This wind'll knock your hat in the creek!" Grandpap said. "Let's tie up the beans before they wind up in Jericho."

With string, we tied runners of bean vines to train them to climb up the poles.

"Do you think Day's Bottom is far?" I asked.

"Depends."

"On what?"

"Where you start from."

I frowned. "That doesn't make sense."

"You could be halfway to Day's Bottom and not even know it," Grandpap said.

I dropped the ball of string, getting steamed under

the collar.

"Which way do I go? East? South? West?" I demanded. "Just answer me one question plain!"

Grandpap heaved a sigh. "I wisht I could, Jane-Ery."

Sometimes Grandpap made me mad. No wonder he never found Day's Bottom. Instead of wondering about where it *might* be, he should have looked for it more.

He chuckled.

"What's so funny?"

"You look like a mule eatin' briars. Just like your mama. When she was a little set-along child, Paulett would get riled at the slightest thing." He glanced up at the pillowy clouds. "Between your face and them clouds, I predict a thunderstorm this afternoon."

"Daddy used to say, 'Threatening clouds oft go around,'" I said.

"Not them clouds. And not that face."

I stalked out of the garden. I didn't know which I

was madder about—him using my face to prophesy bad weather or telling me I looked like Mama.

I didn't go back to the house, knowing Mama would either ride me for getting mad at Grandpap or find a new chore for me. Instead I headed up the mountain. If Grandpap and I weren't going to look for Day's Bottom together, then I'd go look by myself.

Contrary Creek beckoned me to follow it. I took off my shoes and socks and walked in the soft, spongy moss along the bank, thinking about where Day's Bottom might be.

Stood to reason that Day's Bottom had to be at the *bottom* of something, like a valley. Contrary Creek meandered around to the other side of Purgatory Mountain, dropping down into Ghost Eye Holler. Hardly anybody lived there. Not because the holler was haunted (though I secretly thought it was) but because fog usually shrouded its steep slopes till noon.

Daddy took me there once to go swimming. The creek became wide and deep and water splashed over a ledge like a summer shower. Daddy called it a pour-off.

Suppose Day's Bottom was hidden in the swirls of fog that surrounded the little holler? Folks hadn't seen every single thing in these hills, even if they thought they had.

I slipped my wet feet into my shoes, not bothering with my socks, and set off. Too many sticks and rocks in the woods to travel barefoot.

The creek led me up and around, twisting this way and that until it finally made up its mind to go downhill. I locked my knees and took itty-bitty steps to keep from skidding down the mountain on my backside. Years and years of dead leaves were as slippery as fresh snow.

The noise from Contrary Creek grew louder and I knew I was close to the pour-off. Soon I could see it tumble over the rocks, hitting the pool in a white froth.

Below, fog rose like smoke. Or ghosts. Still too early for the sun to reach between the mountains and burn the fog away.

I shredded a fan of locust leaves, hesitating. When I was in the heat of anger at Grandpap, it was fine to take off, show him I didn't need him. But now it didn't seem like such a great idea.

Maybe it would be better to come back when the fog was gone, I told myself.

I didn't want to admit it, but I was afraid of the way the fog shifted, constantly moving. Wisps crept along the ground, wrapping themselves around the trees, rolling over fallen logs.

Then I saw something across the creek, next to a dead chestnut tree, blight-struck like all the chestnuts had been since before I was born. When I stared at the thing, it shimmied away.

I remembered the time Daddy tried to show me the bear den. *Don't look right straight at it*, he'd said. *Kind of glance at it side-like.*

The thing teased back into my line of vision. I turned my head slightly and looked out of the corner of my eyes.

Then I made a small sound.

It wasn't a thing at all. It was a man. He wore brown boots and had longish brown hair, like he needed a haircut.

Daddy.

He'd come back to me. I stretched my arms out and called, "Daddy!" My voice was half-swallowed in the fog and the rush of the pour-off.

But the figure disappeared. His brown boots became the craggy roots of the old chestnut, his hair part of the peeling bark. Then he was gone. There one second, *not there* the next.

Ghost?

The word flew into my head like the thrush-bird that flew into our house once. It thrashed in the corners and flapped against the windowpanes until Mama herded it out with the broom. Mama said a bird in the house was a sign somebody would die.

I didn't believe in ha'nts, as Grandpap called them. My mind must have played a trick on me because I was sorrow-sick.

But suppose Daddy was floating somewhere between heaven and earth? I'd heard of that in Sunday school, especially when people leave this world sudden, like Daddy did.

I shut my eyes and hugged myself. Oh, how I wanted to be with him. I would brave all the ghosts in the Blue Ridge just to walk beside my father again.

A rumbling sound, louder than a bunch of logging trucks, made my eyes fly open. Thunder. It must be dinnertime, at least.

I hurried back up the mountain, brambles snagging my legs. By the time I got home, the towering clouds turned dark as midnight. My sockless shoes had rubbed blisters the size of silver dollars on my heels.

Grandpap was waiting on the porch. He didn't ask where I'd been or why I looked like I'd come out the loser in a catfight. All he said was, "Told you a storm was brewin'."

Thunder boomed around the mountains and high winds lashed rain at our windows.

"Whippoorwill storm," Mama remarked.

"What's that?" I asked. No bird, not even a bird that sat on the woods floor like the whippoorwill, could be out in such weather.

"A spring storm with a lot of wind," Mama replied.

"I heard that sayin' all my life," said Grandpap. "You picked it up from me."

"I reckon I did."

I felt a little sting of jealousy. Mama and Grandpap seemed close, like Daddy and I used to be. A lump of missing-him rose into my throat.

I'd been afraid to think about the vision. Afraid if I took it out and reasoned on it, it would vanish altogether, like a snowflake on a mitten.

Was it the ghost of my father? Did I even believe

in ghosts? Lots of folks along the creek swore up and down that ghosts and witches were real. Exie Dills's aunt Sadie painted her back door blue. Witches only come into a house by the back door, Sadie Dills told me once. And they hate blue.

If that vision was Daddy's ghost, I wasn't afraid. I wanted to see him again, to curl my hand in his, even if his fingers were icy cold.

Grandpap touched a match to a pair of coal-oil lamps. One for Mama. She was piecing him a bed quilt.

Grandpap set the other lamp on the table. Then he went into his room and came out with a box that rustled mysteriously.

"What's in that box?" I asked, rubbing rose salve into my blisters.

"You'll see."

I scooted off the chair and sat cross-legged on the braided rug at Grandpap's feet. I watched as first he threaded a long silver needle. He picked up a bunch of long pine needles and tied the ends together.

Then he began sewing the bundle of pine needles in a coil. His knobby fingers plied the needle over and under until the spiral grew into the bottom of a basket.

"How can you do that?" I asked, turned dreamy-eyed by the movement of his hands.

"My grandma learned me," he said. "She was Cherokee and knew all the old ways. Weaving lets me study on things."

I sifted dried pine needles through my fingers. "What things?"

"Well, like should I buy that sow from Exie Dills? She acts poorly and he's priced her too high."

I was disappointed. I was hoping Grandpap studied on grand things, like were there really and truly angels. Or what made the stars burn and shine.

"Your mama studies on things while she's piecin'," he said. "Don't you, Paulett?"

"Right now I'm studyin' on how many eggs I have to trade for dress goods," she said. "Jane-Ery needs a new dress. I was noticin' on Decoration Day—your green dress is too short."

"Not enough skirt to wad a shotgun," Grandpap added with a wink.

I looked at my mother's head, bent over her quilting hoop. In the lamplight, her gray hairs shone like silver threads and the tight, pinched lines of her face were washed with soft gold.

"I don't need a new dress, Mama," I said, trying to be helpful. If she had one less worry, maybe she wouldn't click her fingernails at night so much.

"Don't tell me what you need or don't need," she said. "You need a new dress for Sunday school."

I sighed. I couldn't win. Deep inside, I really did want a new dress. My green one rode up in the armpits.

As the last grumble of thunder rolled over the mountain, Grandpap laid the finished basket in my lap.

"For you," he said. "For your hair ribbons and

such."

"Thank you!" I rubbed the smooth coiled sides. "Can you teach me how to do this?"

"If you're willin', I'm able."

The next few evenings, while the treefrogs sang, we wove baskets. Grandpap showed me the invisible stitch that makes the basket seem to have no beginning. I learned to loop thread over each coil as I added bundles of long-leaf needles.

My first basket wobbled like a two-legged milking stool, it was so lopsided.

"You'll get better," Grandpap said. "You should have seen my first one. Looked like a cow patty flopped over a rock!"

I laughed till I was stomach-sick.

My second basket was fair looking. It couldn't hold a light to Grandpap's, but I wouldn't have kicked it out of the house.

Grandpap knew all sorts of tricks. He sewed a polished slice of walnut hull into the bottom of a teeny basket. Oh, that basket was a cunning thing, tight-woven and tiny as a baby's fist. He gave it to Mama.

"I want to make one like that," I said. "Like a hummingbird's nest."

"You've got to get weavin' in your hands first," said Grandpap. "Until your fingers do it without thinkin' about it."

My third basket was pretty good, even though I was still thinking too much.

Grandpap made a long basket with Job's tears woven into the handles. The pale gray seeds glowed like pearls against the dark brown of the pine needles.

"What are you going to do with this one?" I asked.

"Give it to whoever happens by," he said.

I touched the polished seeds, seeds that bring good luck, seeds that contain a tiny garden inside, like a kernel of hope.

telling the bees

Every morning, Mama turned a fretful face to the window, studying the sky.

"If it doesn't rain . . . " she began. Then she'd end with "the corn will never tassel" or "the pole limas will wither" or "the cucumbers won't make."

It hadn't rained in over two weeks. Twice a day I carried water to the tomato plants till my arms felt like they were dragging on the ground.

Working the land was so hard. Either there was too much rain or too little, bugs that ate more than we did, and other varmints like groundhogs and deer.

Why didn't we move someplace where life was easier? Like Richmond-city. People in the city didn't sweat and fume over the weather.

"We most always have a dry spell in July," Grandpap said this morning. "Doesn't hurt the squash none. Squash are like weeds. Never gets too dry for either of 'em." He always put a bright face on things.

Mama sat with her chin in her hand, as if giving up on the weather, and said, "You know what? I got a hankerin' for black raspberry cobbler."

"With homemade ice cream?" I added eagerly.

"If you crank."

"I know of a black raspberry bush so thick, you can't find tomorrow in there at midnight," Grandpap said.

"Just so you can find the berries." Mama cleared the table without asking me to, carrying one plate at a time to the drainboard. Lately she'd been doing things like that. Seemed like her mind was somewhere else. Maybe she was tired of working this place, too.

Grandpap and I loaded pails, old clothes, and a poke with our dinner in it in his truck. We drove over to Salter's Mountain, where Grandpap used to live.

I was glad to get out, away from the garden, feeding the hogs, milking Clover. As we rattled up the windy road, a storm of dust flew out from behind our tailgate.

I'd never been to Grandpap's in the summer. Mama, Daddy, and I visited him on Christmas Day. The rest of the time, he came to see us.

"Look!" I pointed through the windshield. A fat black snake at least three feet long stretched across the road. "Don't run him over!"

Grandpap swerved the truck. "I'd never hit a black snake. They're good to have around. Keep rats out of the woodpile."

"Some people kill any kind of snake," I said. "Just for meanness." Once Blue Creedy stomped a little garter snake that was scooting across the playground at school. I called him on it, but he just laughed.

"People go all to pieces when they see a snake," Grandpap said. "They're just plain afraid of 'em. But animals never go out of their way to hurt people, hardly. They're as scared of you as you are of them."

"Even panthers?"

"Jane-Ery, nobody's slapped eyes on a panther since I was a boy." He turned off onto a rutted trace. "And that was a *long* time ago."

"Did you ever see one?"

"No, but my mama used to keep a kettle of water simmering on the fire so panthers wouldn't sneak down the chimney."

The trace led us deep into the woods. Bushes scraped the sides of the truck. I wasn't sure panthers were gone from these parts. I watched out the window, just in case.

Farther down the track I saw a dead possum. His pointy snout showed sharp teeth. His eyes were two empty holes.

I turned away with a shudder.

"Well, his troubles are over," Grandpap remarked lightly.

"He didn't have any eyes."

"Buzzards. Just doin' their job."

I dropped into silence. Whenever my mind had a minute to itself, it turned to what I saw in the holler a few weeks ago. Had I really seen Daddy's ghost? Last night I dreamed it *was* Daddy, come back to make good on his promise to take me to Richmond-city.

We belonged there, Daddy and me. People in the city didn't have to look at dead possums. They wore nice clothes and shiny shoes that never got muddy. They smiled at each other on the streets.

The truck clattered around a bend and the woods opened in a dooryard knee-high with goose grass and careless weed.

Grandpap's mountain was lonesome, but different than the silence on Ghost Eye Holler. Ghost Eye hid secrets in the fog. Salter's Mountain was dead quiet, deserted. I wasn't keen on spending the morning there.

Grandpap switched off the ignition. The engine sputtered a few seconds, then quit. "Remember the old place?" he said.

I nodded. "Yeah. Mama and Daddy and me brought you a jar of oysters on Christmas Day."

Built on stilts, his old-timey cabin leaned against the mountain. A smooth granite slab-rock served as the step to the front porch. Dark uncurtained windows stared back at us like the possum's blank eye sockets.

Grandpap unloaded the back of the truck. "Put on a shirt and pants, Jane-Ery, or them brambles will scratch you to ribbons."

I hopped into a pair of Grandpap's overalls and pulled them right over my dress. I only had to turn the britches-legs up once. I was almost as tall as Grandpap.

"Do you miss your house?" I slipped into one of Daddy's old shirts, burying my nose in the sleeve for a second. A trace of Daddy lingered in the material, like wood smoke on an autumn day.

"I said good-bye to the old place when I left to move in with you-all." He shrugged into a raggedy shirt and buttoned the cuffs.

I glanced over my shoulder. The cabin had a nice, solid look, as if it had been carved out of the mountain itself. I think I would have missed it, a little.

The black raspberry bushes were behind the cabin, past Grandpap's overgrown garden. Canes bowed over, heavy with fruit.

"Looks like we beat the birds," Grandpap said.

We each staked out a patch and commenced picking. Thorns raked my hands as I reached deeper to pull off the juiciest, ripest berries. I liked the soft *plunk* the berries made when I dropped them into my pail. I ate a bunch, too.

"These berries don't add up like blackberries," I said. Blackberries were plumper and filled the pail quicker.

"No, but black raspberries have a taste all their own."

The sun blazed down. I bet it was hotter on
Grandpap's mountain than anyplace on earth, even
Araby.

When our pails were full, we sat under a persimmon tree and ate our dinner. A squirrel draped himself over a branch, all four feet dangling. He didn't
twitch a whisker at our presence.

"Even the squirrel's hot," I said, shedding my shirt
and overalls.

"Sun's at its peak this time of year," Grandpap said.
"Six months from now you'll be cravin' some of this
hot weather."

Six months from now. I couldn't think that far
ahead. Would I still be missing Daddy so much?
Would Mama find money to pay our bills?

We took the pails back to the truck.

"I have to do something before we head home,"
Grandpap said.

"What?"

"You'll see."

We walked around the far side of the cabin, past the pump, past the privy.

A beehive stood on a wooden platform near the grassy slope. Bees buzzed around the hive. I heard humming inside.

I hung back. I was afraid of bees. But Grandpap stepped right up to the hive.

"What are you going to do?" I asked. He was making me nervous.

Grandpap fished in his baggy overalls pocket and took out a brass door key. Holding the key out in front of him, he moved closer to the hive and bent down. Bees swooped around his head, but he didn't flinch.

"Sorry I didn't get here sooner," he said to the hive. "I hope you-all understand. My daughter's husband was kilt in an accident the first of April. I moved down there to be with my daughter and my granddaughter, Jane-Ery. That's her right over there."

I couldn't believe my ears. Grandpap was talking

to the beehive! Just like the bees were people!

He straightened up. "That's it for this year. I hope you'll stay." He put the key back in his pocket and walked away from the hive.

I ran back to the truck, certain a mob of angry bees was zooming after us. Grandpap took his sweet time, whistling "Pretty Polly."

We climbed in the truck, and Grandpap drove back down the lane.

Mama said people sometimes got childish in their old age. I didn't know how old Grandpap was. He had young-looking eyes, so it was hard to tell. I wondered if talking to beehives with a door key in his hand was a sign of becoming childish.

Grandpap must have read my mind. "No, I'm not off my box. I had to tell the bees the news so they wouldn't swarm and leave the hive."

"What news?"

"The house news." He looked over at me. "Bees are members of the family, you know. You can't treat 'em just any ol' way. They're prideful critters. They like to know what's going on."

"So you told them about Daddy?"

"You tell the bees about a baby or somebody's passin'. Or if somebody in the family got married. It's tradition."

It sounded like a strange tradition to me. "What do the bees do if you don't?"

"Leave," he said. "You have to tell 'em around swarmin' time—May, June. July at the very latest. If you show 'em the door key, they won't go off."

"Do you get honey from those bees?" I asked.

"Yep. Missed the sourwood season, though. Right around Independence Day the sourwoods are in full bloom. Purty little flowers called angel fingers."

Angel fingers. How I loved Grandpap's fanciful words. What would angel fingers feel like, I wondered.

He went on. "Sourwood trees make the best honey in the world. Like liquid gold." He smacked his lips. "Nettie kept a glass dish of honey settin' on the table.

So we could reach over and dig up a big spoonful any-time."

"How did you get the honey from the bees?" I asked.

"Rob the hive with a smokin' torch."

My skin crawled at the thought. "I bet you got stung a lot."

"Oncet or twicet. If you act scairt, bees know it. That's when they sting."

"It still seems funny," I said. "Telling the bees about Daddy, I mean." Why would bees care about my father?

"There's something meaningful in telling the bees," Grandpap said. "They carry pollen so plants grow. Even though a person comes to the end of their life, bees make sure life goes on."

When we got home, Mama was on the porch bust-ing a burlap sack of ice with a hammer.

"I would of gone to Exie's for the ice," Grandpap told her.

"He dropped by. When I said I was making ice cream, he skittered home and brought ice back so fast, my last words were still in the air."

Exie Dills kept ice packed in sawdust in his root cellar. He was a fool for Mama's ice cream, so I knew he'd be back later.

Mama handed me the hammer. "Here, Jane-Ery. Pap, will you clean the ice cream maker? I got to check on the custard."

I whacked ice till my arms ached from the cold. Then I went inside to help Mama. I rinsed the berries while she mixed lard and flour and table sugar for the cobbler. Mama added berries to the ice cream, turning the custard a pretty purply-pink. She put the cobbler in the oven. I held the metal canister with its dasher while Mama poured the custard in.

Grandpap had laid out the parts of the ice cream maker on the porch. Mama set the metal canister down in the wooden tub. Then she packed crushed ice around the canister, added rock salt to the ice, and clamped on the hand crank.

"I turn first," I said.

Sitting on the edge of the porch, I cranked the handle. The canister spun around in the ice.

"Mama, I'm worried about Grandpap."

"Why? What happened?" Her voice sharpened with concern. Her own worry was never far from the surface.

"After we picked berries, he talked to the bees in his beehive," I said. "He told them about Daddy. Is he getting childish?"

Mama smiled, the first real smile I'd seen from her in weeks. It was like the sun breaking through evening clouds.

"No, Jane-Ery. Pap is not childish. And he's not talkin' moonlight, neither. Pap's been tellin' the bees the doin's in our family since I can remember. It's a tradition."

"That's what he said. Grandpap sure has funny ways, doesn't he?"

"No funnier than most." She tipped the tub to drain the melted ice water. "My people are superstitious, so I'm used to it."

"What's superstitious?" I said, stumbling over the word.

"Believing in good luck and bad luck." She added more ice and salt. "Like not putting a hat on the bed. I had a aunt who would no more put her bonnet on the bed than fly to the moon. She thought she would get bad luck if she did. I don't put my hat on the bed, neither."

"Are you afraid of bad luck?"

Mama saw the churning was getting harder so she took over. "I don't think it hurts to believe a little in bad luck *and* good luck. Taking after my family keeps them close to my heart, even though most of 'em are gone."

I wondered if people in Richmond-city were afraid to put a hat on the bed. Did they tell the bees their news? I doubted it. They were too citified.

Exie Dills showed up as soon as Mama pronounced the ice cream ready.

"Exie," said Grandpap. "You must have some kind of ice cream radar, like the airplane fellers use."

"Take the good rocker," Mama told Exie. "And pay Pap no mind. Jane-Ery, bring out the soup plates, spoons, and the cobbler. Don't burn yourself."

Mama dished up slabs of cobbler topped with huge scoops of ice cream.

Exie took one bite and said, "Paulett, you make the best ice cream in the county."

"Her cobbler ain't no patch on her mama's, neither," said Grandpap. "And folks claimed Nettie's cobbler was the best in the county."

I ate my ice cream too fast and got shooting pains behind my eyes. I squinched my eyes shut till the pains passed.

"You're gobblin' like a registered hog," said Grandpap.

"We don't have ice cream that often," I said.

"All the more reason to eat it slow," said Exie. "It's like life. People are in such an all-fired hurry these days."

We sat on the porch, eating and talking, until the swallows twittered overhead.

"Soon be dark," Exie said, heaving himself out of the rocker. "Better light a shuck for home."

"You have headlights on your truck," I told him. He didn't need a torch to light his way.

He laughed. "I know, Jane-Ery. I intend to use 'em."

Mama and Grandpap walked him to his pickup. They talked some more in that hard-to-let-go way grown-ups have.

I strolled across our dooryard, thinking about to-morrow. I wanted to go to Ghost Eye Holler again. Should I ask Grandpap to go with me? Would he make fun of me if I told him I'd seen Daddy there?

Beneath my bare toes, the clover was cool and damp. More than once, I'd stepped on a honeybee. I hopped on one foot to the house, crying. Mama had smacked wet tobacco on the sting. I bet folks in Richmond would laugh at that.

A lone bee droned low over the ground, headed

somewhere. He was such a small critter, he didn't even see me. Now I know what Grandpap meant about animals not aiming to hurt people. They were just going about their business.

I squatted down in the grass. Don't act scared, Grandpap had said.

"Hello, bee. I bet you're heading home to bed. I just want to tell you the news. My—" I swallowed hard. "My daddy was kilt when logs fell off a truck."

The bee's hum sounded sympathetic. Maybe he cared after all.

We were clearing up the dishes when it sounded like hickory nuts hitting the roof.

"Rain!" I said.

The racket grew louder.

"A real toad-strangler," Grandpap remarked.

"Rain like this will beat the tomatoes in the ground," Mama said, switching to a new worry.

"We can stake 'em back up," Grandpap told her.

Then he asked, "Did we eat all the biscuits for sup-per?"

"Every last one," Mama told him.

"Fair day tomorrow, then," he said with a wink at me.

Predicting weather by biscuits? Maybe Grandpap was talking moonlight. Then again, maybe he wasn't.

like meat loves salt

All of a sudden, the garden raced ahead of us. Tomato plants bent double with red globes, the corn tasseled, and we couldn't step out the door without a bucket to fill with beans or squash or cucumbers.

Grandpap worked from can't-see to can't-see. Mama put up beans and beets, blackberries and peaches. The pressure cooker simmered on the stove all day. I washed lids and rings and tried to stay out of Mama's way.

Mason jars lined the drainboard in rows. Through the clear glass jars, I admired the neat-cut beans, the bright purples of beets and berries. At night, the *snap! pop!* of lids sealing broke into my dreams.

Then one August day, Mama turned from the stove, her face redder than the vinegar beets she had just canned.

"Enough," she said. "I need to get out of this heat. Jane-Ery, fetch that basket of eggs." She went into Grandpap's room and came out with a box of corn shuck foot mats. She had plaited them last winter.

"What are you doing with that stuff?" I asked.

"Bartering." She went to the door and called, "Pap! Can you run us to Parson's?"

Grandpap was glad of a break from weeding. Soon we were jouncing down the mountain road. Mama held the egg basket on her lap and a determined look around her mouth.

At Parson's Store, an overhead fan stirred the stuffy air in lazy circles. Yellow flypaper dangling from it was dotted with fly carcasses.

Mama marched up to the counter and said to Burt

Parson, "What'll you give me for these in trade for dress goods?"

Grandpap lifted the box of foot mats onto the counter. I set the egg basket next to the box.

"Material for me! Can I pick it out, Mama?" I wanted something pretty. *Not* green calico.

Grandpap led me away from the counter. "How about a cold soda pop?" He dropped a nickel into the cooler and lifted the lid.

I leaned inside the cooler, drinking in the delicious chill, and pondered my choices. Orange Crush or Grape Ne-Hi? I loved them both. Orange Crush had more bite, but the Grape Ne-Hi was sweeter.

Finally I plunged my hand into the icy water and pulled out the grape. Grandpap whacked off the cap. I tilted the bottle and drank.

"Want some?" I offered my drink to Grandpap.

He shook his head. "It's all your'n."

"Is my tongue purple?" I stuck my tongue out.

"Like a skink's."

I giggled. The quick little lizards that darted around our porch had the purplest tongues.

"Jane-Ery." Mama crooked her finger at me. "Come here."

I hustled to the front of the store. Mama had laid out five or six bolts of material on the counter.

"Which of these do you like?" she asked.

They were all calico, printed with little flowers. Every dress I'd ever had was calico. I looked up at the shelf where Mr. Parson kept the dress goods.

"I like that one." I pointed to a pink-and-white check.

Mr. Parson brought the pink check over to the counter. He unwound a length of the fabric and draped it over my shoulder. Once Mama said Mr. Parson acted like he was running a fancy department store in the flatlands.

"Pink suits you, Jane-Ery," he said.

Mama flipped the material off me. "I'll decide what suits her or not." She gave me a good long look. Then she said, "Pink does suit you. How much, Burt?"

"Only twenty-nine cents more than the calico," Mr. Parson said.

"Let me have four yards."

While he measured the cloth, Mama picked out pink and white spool-thread and pink buttons.

"Mama?" I held out a pack of pink rickrack.

"All right. But that's it." She put the notions on the counter. "Times I recall when buying fotched-on cloth was something special. My mother grew her own flax and wove linen. When we got hold of calico, with every color in the rainbow, we thought we'd died and flew to heaven."

Fotched-on. Sometimes my mother sounded like Grandpap. I was sure people in Richmond-city said "store-bought." After all, they had those fancy stores that advertised on the radio.

As Mama picked up the package with my new material in it, I looked at her hands. I'd never really noticed hairline marks along the sides of her fingers.

Fine, red scars from plaiting all those corn shucks.

I ran my thumbnail along a lima bean shell, zipped it open, and plopped fat beans into the dishpan clamped between my knees. The heaping bushel Grandpap had picked earlier hadn't gone down a hair.

"I hate hulling limas," I complained. "The shells are tough as shoe leather."

"But you like eating your mama's creamed limas and corn?" Grandpap asked. He had pulled the spark plugs from his pickup and was cleaning them with his case knife. Like Mama's, Grandpap's hands were never still.

I didn't have to answer. He knew I heaped my plate every time Mama fixed them.

Garden work never seemed to end. Weeding, hoeing, picking, shucking, shelling, putting up . . . I was fair tired of it. But Mama told me to hull these limas before going to bed.

If Daddy were here, he'd say, Jane-Ery's done enough today. He'd hull those beans before you could say Jack

Sprat. And let me go wading in the creek till dark.

At least it wasn't so hot on the porch. None of us could hardly eat supper—the kitchen was an oven.

"I bet it's nice and cool in Day's Bottom," I said.

"Like the swimming hole in May."

I wiped my face on my dresstail. "I wisht I could go there now. I wisht I could go swimming instead of shelling these ol' beans."

"No point wishin' your life away," Grandpap said. "Look what happened to that king."

"What king?"

"Just a king back in the olden days."

"Oh. This is one of your stories." I settled back.

Grandpap cleared his throat. "Long ever ago, there lived a king with three daughters. One day he said to them, 'I'm going to town. What you like me to buy you?' The eldest daughter wanted a fancy red dress. The second daughter wanted a fancy green dress. And the youngest daughter, all she wanted was a plain white dress."

I wondered why the youngest daughter gave up a chance for a pretty dress. When I got to Day's Bottom, I planned to wear a different party dress every day.

"The king got on his horse and went to town. He bought the dresses and rode home. Then he called his daughters in one by one. He asked the eldest, 'How much do you love me?'

"She said, 'I love you more than life.' The king gave her the red dress.

"Next he asked the second daughter, 'How much do you love me?'

"She said, 'I love you more than I can tell you.' The king gave her the green dress.

"Last, he asked the younger daughter, 'How much do you love me?'

"She said, 'I love you like meat loves salt.'

"The king got mad at her answer. He said he wished she would go away, and he didn't give her the white dress. Brokenhearted, she left home. She married a prince far away and beyond.

"Years later," Grandpap said, "when the king was old and blind, he went to live with his eldest daughter. She said there wasn't room for his servants and sent them away. Then the king went to live with his second daughter. She made him sleep in the barn. He knew then his daughters didn't really love him."

I gripped the sides of my pan. "What about the youngest daughter?"

"She found the old king and took him in. But he didn't know her. So one night she cooked a mess of side meat and kale without any salt. The king took a bite and said it didn't taste right. His daughter brung him a dish of salt." Grandpap paused. "Suddenly the old king knew her. She was the daughter who loved him true. He gave her the white dress and they all lived happy."

"I like that story," I said. The bushel basket was empty except for a few withered stems and leaves in the bottom. I was listening so hard, I never noticed.

Grandpap stretched his legs. "I'm ready to hit the sack. Tomorrow will come soon enough." He twisted around to look through the kitchen window. "The day hasn't ended for your mama, though."

I turned and looked, too.

Mama had cleared the table and spread out my pink check cloth. With a mouth full of pins, she smoothed the wrinkled tissue pattern and pinned the pieces to the cloth. Before she went to bed, I knew she'd cut out my dress and stitch the seams.

My heart felt funny, like an old rubber ball that had lost its bounce. I loved my daddy more than anyone on earth. He was the only person who never found fault with me.

I never told Daddy how much I loved him. We didn't talk about such, any more than we did a lot of hugging or kissing. We were loving-like in other ways.

What if something happened to Mama, too? I'd hate myself if I didn't let her know I was proud to be her daughter.

But if I told Mama I loved her like meat loves salt, she'd say, "Jane-Ery, you're crazy as a hoot owl."

wishing on the new moon

I slipped out of the house, easing the door latch. Mama was finally snoring and Grandpap wasn't awake yet. Only the mockingbird, who'd been screeching and singing from the ridgepole of the shed, saw me. He jerked his tail and glared at me with one beady eye.

"Don't let me keep you up," I said sarcastically. The stupid bird had been singing all night for over a week. Mama and I both felt rough as a corncob from lack of sleep. But Grandpap said the mockingbird got good reception from our shed roof, like the antenna on the top of the mountain.

The sun hadn't peeked through the early-morning fog yet. Though my mouth felt like the bottom of a chicken coop, I knew this was the only time I could steal from the day. I had to go back to Ghost Eye Holler.

My feet found the path to Contrary Creek. The stream chuckled along beside me. Soon the ground pitched downward and I stilt-walked down the steep slope. The pour-off flumed over rocks, splashing me.

Ghost Eye Holler was as still as a graveyard. No sparrows peeped. No squirrels scampered through the leaves.

Heavy fog wreathed the trees, trailing like white scarves. A whole army of ghosts could be hiding in that soup.

"Daddy?" I said, my voice muffled. "Are you here?"

The fog shifted, parting to reveal a rotted stump, a craggy rock, a fallen poplar like a giant from one of Grandpap's stories—then covering them up again. It was as if those things never existed.

"Daddy?" I said again, louder this time. My voice stopped short, landing about a foot in front of me.

My lungs squeezed. What if the fog swallowed me up and I disappeared like the stump and the rock? I could almost feel wispy fingers draping around my throat, pulling me forward.

This place couldn't lead to Day's Bottom. I didn't know why I saw Daddy here the last time, but he wasn't here now.

I turned and scrabbled up the hill, scraping my bare toes on stony outcroppings. Contrary Creek rushed by in the opposite direction as if to say, *Jane-Ery, you're going the wrong way.*

By the time I reached home, smoke from the woodstove puffed its welcome. Grandpap was up. He'd have the coffee perking and Mama would be fixing breakfast. I'd just tell them I got up to take a walk, that was all.

Before I went inside, I glanced back in the direction of the creek. Maybe I'd made up seeing Daddy the other time.

Maybe, I thought, he was just a heart-wish.

"Won't you come?" I asked Mama. "Please?"

Mama sliced a cucumber. The kitchen smelled strong after vinegar. "I have to finish these pickles, Jane-Ery."

"Exie Dills invited you 'specially."

"Tell Exie I'm sorry, but the cucumbers won't wait."

Mama didn't visit anybody these days. After Decoration Day, she wouldn't go back to church or see any of her friends. When Exie Dills asked us to come down and listen to his radio, Mama suddenly decided to make a batch of seven-day pickles.

"You don't mind if Grandpap and I go?" I asked, twirling in my new dress. It was prettier than the fancy dresses the king's daughters asked him to buy in town.

"No point in all of us stayin' home. Wipe the table

off first."

I swiped a rag over the oilcloth. Another envelope was tucked under the sugar bowl. I glanced over at Mama. She wasn't looking in my direction.

Quick as a black snake, I flicked the envelope out just a little so I could read the return address. *Amherst County Treasurer*. This bill was stamped *Past Due*, too.

Why did Mama owe money to the county treasurer? Was she in trouble?

Grandpap came into the kitchen. "Ready?"

"Yeah."

We walked down Contrary Creek to our neighbor's house. Grandpap hummed his happy-go-lucky tune, as Mama called it, making it up as he went along. Sometimes he pushed the notes between his teeth in little buzzes. I wondered how he could be so cheerful when Mama owed money to the county.

Exie's dooryard was covered with rusted car parts and hubcaps. Sweetlips, his old hunting dog, snoozed under an old wringer washing machine. The dog thumped his tail in greeting but did not stir himself.

Exie met us on the porch. He wore suspenders over a red shirt and boots with holes punched over the toes to give his corns "breathin' air."

"Hi-dy." He led us into the front room. "Draw up a chair and cool off. I'll get us something to drink."

Grandpap and I shifted piles of yellowed newspapers so we could sit down.

I picked up one of the newspapers, *The Richmond-Times Dispatch*, only a year old. I turned the page to a drawing of a lady in a skirt so wide, she'd never fit through a barn door. She wore white gloves and held a china cup with her pinky finger crooked. "The next time you're shopping in Thalheimers, refresh yourself in our tearoom," it said below the picture.

I imagined myself in that magical place, refreshing myself in the Thalheimers tearoom. Outside, I'd see the city, bright with electric lights and filled with fancy stores and friendly people at every turn. Grandpap called them flatlanders, but at least they didn't have to scratch for a living. Cityfolk danced at play-parties and ate in restaurants, like the lady holding the teacup. I could tell she never hulled a lima with her pretty gloved hands. I craved to be like her.

Exie came back with two sweating glasses of lemonade. "I never throw nothin' away. That's how come me to have so many newspapers. Burt Parson saves 'em for me. I like to keep up on things." He handed me one of the glasses.

"Thank you," I said. The glass wasn't any none too clean, but, as Daddy always said, a little dirt never kilt anybody.

"Lemonade is a real treat," said Grandpap.

"Remember Independence Day at the orchard?" Exie asked Grandpap. "I used to make the lemonade. Chip ice from the ice block under the mill. Squeeze them ol' lemons." He raised his voice. "'Ice cold lemonade! Made in the shade, stirred with a spade! Best lemonade that's ever been made!'"

"You don't memorize the chestnut orchard,"

Grandpap said to me. "The blight kilt all the trees before you were born. But back then, it was the best place to celebrate the Fourth."

I didn't want to listen to talk about the old days. "Can we play the radio now?"

"All you have to do is ask." Exie switched on his battery radio and fiddled with the dial.

WRVA blared through the speaker loud at first, then faint, like a train winding through mountains. Exie adjusted the tuner until the station came in good.

A girl sang, "How much is that dog-gie in the window?" I liked her singing voice, but the words didn't make sense. Why would anybody buy a dog from a store? Dogs were as plentiful as jar flies in August.

When the song was over, an excitable-sounding woman jabbered about a dish soap that made pink bubbles and gave her smooth hands. Mama didn't believe in wasting good money on store-bought dish soap, but I wouldn't mind washing dishes in a sinkful of pink bubbles.

The radio announcer said, "This is WRVA, Richmond's own station. Our next tune will be from America's favorite crooner, Bing Crosby."

"Ever been to Richmond-city?" I asked Exie.

"Oncet," he replied. "I took a girl to the picture show. That was back when I was sparkin'. I got so tangled up in all them streets, thought I'd never spy daylight again."

I had never been to the pictures, but other people on Purgatory Mountain had. "Did you like the show?"

"Never found the movie-house! And the girl—Dora Jean, it was, you remember her, Willard—she puffed up like a bullfrog and called me a durned ol' fool." Exie chuckled at the memory. "Reckon I was."

If I went to Richmond-city, I'd walk down those streets in my new pink dress like I owned them. I wouldn't be the least little bit scared. I'd take Mama and we'd go to the picture show. We'd have a high old time and wouldn't worry about any past-due bills.

After a while, Grandpap said it was time we'd headed up the hill. He stood up like Daddy did when he was ready to leave. No lingering.

Exie walked us to the door. "Come on back for supper sometime. I'll cook the dishrag if I can't find nothing else. Tell your mama I said hey, Jane-Ery." His voice got soft when he said "mama."

"I will. Thanks for the lemonade."

We took the path along the creek. The sky had gone dusky-dark. Bats flitted overhead, chirping and snatching gnats on the wing.

"Do you think Exie likes Mama?" I asked Grandpap.

"You mean, is he settin' his cap for her?" Grandpap sounded thoughtful. "Hard to say. His wife run off years ago. Only wrote oncet to say she got a di-vorce. I 'spect Exie gets right lonesome."

Maybe Mama knew that and that was why she didn't come. I didn't want to think about Exie Dills or anybody else setting their cap for my mother.

"Are there picture shows at Day's Bottom?" I asked Grandpap, changing the subject.

"Day's Bottom has anything a body would ever want," he answered.

"Anything?" I asked doubtfully. "How can one place have anything anybody would ever want?"

"It just does."

There he went again. Why couldn't he answer one question about Day's Bottom sensible-like? I walked ahead in a huff.

"You're mighty impatient tonight," Grandpap said, catching up.

Usually I love listening to Exie's radio, but tonight I felt agitated.

"I saw a bill under the sugar bowl," I told him. "From the county treasurer, stamped past due. Is Mama in trouble?"

Grandpap didn't answer for a few seconds. "Some things you aren't supposed to see, Jane-Ery."

"It was in plain sight on the kitchen table."

"I meant, it's grown-up business."

"If I'm old enough to work, I'm old enough to know about what's going on," I said stubbornly. "Is Mama in trouble with the county?"

"No," he said. "Your mama is lagging behind in paying the property tax."

"I thought we owned our land. Daddy said his daddy gave him the homeplace."

"He did. But even if you own land outright, you still have to pay taxes on it every year. Since your daddy died—well, your mama's been short of cash-money."

I knew that right along. "How much does Mama owe?"

"Two hundred and fourteen dollars," Grandpap replied. "And eighty-three cents."

Two hundred and fourteen dollars. And eighty-three cents. It might as well be two million dollars.

"Will Mama have to get a job?" I asked, my worries tumbling out. "Will she leave the holler like Arizona

Creedy to clean rooms?"

Motels had sprouted like toadstools after a rain-storm in the foothills of the Blue Ridge Parkway, the big road that wound through the mountains. Arizona made good money. She even bought herself a blue plastic pocketbook and a wallet to match. She carried the pocketbook to church every Sunday and made a show of opening it when the collection plate came down her pew.

"Your mama isn't going nowhere," Grandpap said. "Things will work out. They always do. Look up there."

He pointed to the skinniest moon-sliver hanging in the deepening sky.

"Make a wish over your left shoulder," he said.

"Why?"

"It's good luck to wish on the new moon."

I bit my lip. "I don't know. . . ."

"Another night and old man moon will be flat on his back," said Grandpap. "Too late for wish-makin'."

I thought about Arizona's blue pocketbook. When she closed it, the clasp made a rich-sounding *chunk*. Should I wish for a pocketbook?

Then I thought about that two hundred and fourteen dollars and eighty-three cents. I should wish for that instead. It would be worth it to have Mama quit worrying her fingernails like a string of Job's tears.

"Wish big," Grandpap said.

But I could find plenty of money in Day's Bottom. Anything anybody would ever want is in Day's Bottom, according to Grandpap.

Maybe, I thought, *I should ask the way to Day's Bottom, instead.*

I twisted around so I could see the moon over my left shoulder, closed my eyes, and wished away.

Big.

walking in the wind

Fall-time came. I went back to school in my old green calico dress and my old brown lace-up shoes. Inside my skin I felt different. When other kids made over me, I couldn't be bothered with them.

The leaves turned red and yellow before gusty winds ripped them away. Songbirds headed south like the flying leaves. Great gaggles of them lit on the treetops, squawking and jabbering in a hundred different voices, like the Tower of Babel. Then, as if by signal, they all flew up again in a fluttery rush of wings.

Toting burlap sacks, Grandpap and I hiked up Purgatory Mountain.

"When I was a boy," he said, "I saw whistling swans across the new moon. *Woo-hoo, woo-hoo,* the leader halloed. Little swans flew between the bigger birds. Those birds go so fast, the young'uns were pulled right along. Ever' time I heard them, I was helped up"

"How come I've never seen swans?" I asked.

"You have to be at exactly the right place."

I wanted to see the swans. "Where is it? Can we go there now?"

"We've got something more important to do today," he said.

Purple flowers Mama called farewell-summer brushed against our legs as we climbed the trail. Grandpap's step was keen as creek water. I had trouble keeping up with him.

The woods were cool and quiet. I crashed through underbrush, half lost in a daydream.

"You make more noise than a mule in a tin shed,"

Grandpap said.

We stopped at a mammoth walnut tree. Its branches seemed to scrape the sky.

"That tree's so tall," he said, "we'll have to lay down to spy the top."

A walnut rolled under my shoe. The soft green husk had been gnawed open by a squirrel. My foot twisted under, and the husk left a brown stain on my tennis shoe.

"Let's fill these sacks," Grandpap said, handing me a pair of work gloves. Daddy's.

Daddy's gloves didn't fit, but I slipped them on anyway. My fingers wiggled inside sweat-blackened leather and I imagined his hands holding mine again.

"Where are your gloves?" I asked. Daddy's gloves didn't fit, but I wore them anyway.

"A little stain won't hurt my old fingers."

While we picked walnuts, Grandpap told me about when he was a boy.

"I walked two miles to school," he said. "Carried

my lunch in a King's syrup pail."

"What did you eat?" I asked. I liked bologna sandwiches, but Mama didn't buy bologna much.

"Cornbread crumbled in buttermilk," he said. "Sometimes a cathead biscuit with a slice of hammeat."

"What is a cathead biscuit?"

"What it sounds like," he said. "Biscuit big as a tomcat's head. Need two hands to hold 'em."

"Did you like school?"

"I'druther be huntin'," Grandpap said. "One time I wanted to go squirrel huntin.' So I crawled out the schoolhouse window when the teacher wasn't looking."

"What happened?"

"Fell plumb-dab in a patch of poison oak! While I was fightin' to get out of the weeds, I tangled with a black snake!"

I pictured Grandpap and a black snake thrashing in poison oak and laughed. "What did your teacher do?"

"Blistered my backside with the Board of Education," he answered. "That cured me of any more window-crawlin'. I still didn't like school, though."

"I don't mind school," I said. Geography was my best subject. In class, I pored over the atlas, hoping I'd stumble on Day's Bottom.

"Your father told me oncet you were good at book-readin'," Grandpap said. "He was always braggin' on you."

Tears burned my eyes like I was peeling ramps. My eyes ached from squeezing the tears back.

"He'd be proud of you," said Grandpap.

"How?" I asked. "How can he be proud of me? He doesn't know what I'm doing."

"Oh, yes, he does. He's watchin' you right now. He sees you've grown a couple inches since spring. He sees your hair shinin' in the sun. He thinks you're as purty as a new-laid robin's egg."

"I don't believe you. Daddy is dead." Or was he? For

weeks, I'd turned over the thought that he still lingered here on earth. I hadn't told anyone about seeing him in Ghost Eye Holler. Who'd believe me, especially since he didn't show himself when I went back?

"Your father is gone," Grandpap said softly. "But he isn't dead in your heart and mind."

I set my mouth in a straight line. Grandpap didn't know anything about what was in my heart and mind.

We picked walnuts in silence. When the bags bulged, Grandpap took our last empty sack into a piney part of the woods. Long pine needles were scattered on the ground like straw.

"This is the best time to collect them," he said. "The needles are hard and shiny and a nice shade of brown. Leave them a season, they get too brittle and dull to use for baskets."

We filled the sack with enough needles to make baskets till the hereafter.

Then Grandpap rested against the walnut tree, his bony hands lying in his lap.

My feet found the path Daddy and I used to take on our after-supper rambles.

Over the fallen log, around the rock that looked like a sleeping dog, up to the old flume. I hadn't been up here since Daddy died.

Not a single bird whistled. No chipmunks rustled in the leaves.

I stood perfectly still in the quiet.

Oh, Daddy, I thought.

Waves of sorrow rippled through me, like a stone tossed in a pond. Would the hurt ever go away? The pain wasn't as sharp as before Grandpap came, but it still caught me unawares. I'd be shucking corn or hauling water to the hogs, not thinking about anything in particular, when—*wham!* That old hurt would slam into me, knock the breath out of my chest.

I closed my eyes and wished the pain away.

Jane-Ery.

I opened my eyes.

He leaned against a silver maple, grinning at me. He looked different than he did in Ghost Eye Holler. Maybe it was because no fog shrouded him. Somehow I expected him to be wearing his funeral suit. The one he wore to other people's funerals. The one he was buried in.

Rolled-up shirt sleeves showed his strong, tanned arms. His broken bootlaces were tied in knots. I remember the day before he was kilt, Mama promised to get him new bootlaces at Parson's. And his hair needed trimming.

He didn't look the least bit dead. He looked so real, hope leaped into my heart.

"Daddy!" But my voice came out in a whisper.

Then Daddy grew shimmery and soft along the edges, like the moon on a hazy night. He stopped grinning. His eyes looked sad.

"Don't take on so, Jane-Ery," he said.

Or I thought he said. Maybe I heard it in my head. And then he was gone, leaving me staring at the smooth trunk of the silver maple.

"Daddy?"

He did not answer.

This time I knew I saw him. But where did he go? Why didn't he stay and talk to me? I had so much to say to him.

Grandpap was right about one thing. Daddy wasn't dead in my heart and mind. Daddy hadn't left at all. He was too much of a *person* to be gone in an eyeblink.

It was clear to me that Daddy was trying to tell me something. That he couldn't stay on Purgatory Mountain anymore. He had to move on. And I knew where.

Grandpap had said anything anybody wanted was at Day's Bottom. What I wanted more than anything, more than a blue plastic pocketbook, more than penny candy, more than money to pay the tax bill, even, was to have my father back.

All I had to do was find Day's Bottom. There, we'd

be together again.

I felt better, then. Daddy had a saying for feeling dreamy-good. "Walking in the wind," he called it.

I walked in the wind all the way back to the walnut tree.

halfway

Back home, Grandpap drove his truck over the walnuts to roll the husks off. Then he poured buckets of water in our apple butter kettle and stirred the unshelled nuts around. Next we spread the washed nuts on a canvas sheet and let them dry in the October sun.

"What are you going to do with all these walnuts?" I asked.

"Sell them," said Grandpap.

"Down at Parson's?"

Grandpap shook his head. "Not Parson's. The market in Richmond-city."

Richmond-city! My pulse jumped. Suddenly I knew, the way a baby chick knows when it's time to come out of the egg, where Day's Bottom was.

"Can I go with you! Please? Oh, please!"

"If your mama says so—"

I flew into the house where Mama was fixing supper. My words spilled over. "Mama, Grandpap is going to Richmond-city to sell the walnuts. Can I go with him? Please? Daddy was going to take me on my birthday, remember, Mama?"

"Yes, Jane-Ery, I remember."

"Well, can I?"

"We'll see." Her tone told me I couldn't argue anymore.

When Grandpap came inside to eat, I asked, "When are you going to Richmond-city?"

"Not yet awhile. Won't be till after Thanksgiving. Folks like fresh black walnuts around holiday time."

Thanksgiving! I didn't think I'd live that long.

But chores and schoolwork kept me busy. At the

first hard freeze, Grandpap and Exie Dills kilt our hogs. Mama put up fresh sausage patties, packing them in jars between layers of lard. After supper, Grandpap and I wove baskets by the stove.

Exie Dills stopped by more often, to bring us a rabbit he'd trapped or to help Grandpap stack wood on our porch. Once he admired a basket Grandpap had just finished.

"This sorry-lookin' thing?" Grandpap turned the beautiful oval basket in his hands. He had used pine needles dried in the shade, which gave them a greenish cast. "If you want it, you can have it," he told Exie. "But put it away if anybody happens by. I'd be ashamed for folks to see it."

"You stubborn old fool," Exie said with a grin. "You know this basket could take the blue ribbon at the state fair."

When he left, I said to Grandpap, "Exie's right. Nobody makes better baskets than you. Why don't you sell them instead of giving them away? I bet people would pay big money."

"Giving my baskets away keeps joy in my heart," he replied.

But it didn't pay the past-due tax bill, I thought.

At long last it was December. Grandpap dragged the walnut bags from the spring house where he had stored them. With a mallet he cracked walnuts right in the bag.

Mama and I sorted the broken pieces and picked out the oily nutmeats. Then we scooped them into clean feed sacks. By the time we finished hours later, my fingers were cramped.

When I saw Grandpap gassing up his pickup, I knew he was fixing to leave on a long trip.

"You're going to Richmond-city to sell the walnuts, aren't you?" I whirled around to face Mama. "Can I go too? Pretty please?"

"We'll see."

"You said that the last time!"

"You have to get up early," Grandpap said, as if it had already been decided.

"I will!"

"You help your grandfather," Mama said.

"Grandpap won't have to lift a finger!" I would have promised everything under the sun, moon, and stars just to go.

"You driving too?" Grandpap asked with a wink.

I thudded into my room and fished my best basket from under the bed. Grandpap and Mama were still sorting walnuts and didn't see me hide a paper bag inside the truck. Grandpap wouldn't sell his baskets, but I'd sell *mine*.

Before the sun was out of bed, Grandpap and I were riding in his rattly old truck.

Frost-fog webbed the hills as we drove through the gap.

"See that fog?" Grandpap said. "That's steam from groundhogs making coffee."

I could barely sit still. Soon I'd see Daddy waiting for me on a Richmond street corner. He'd say, "Jane-Ery, you look mighty pretty in that pink dress. We never did celebrate your birthday. Let's take in a picture show."

"How long before we get there?" I asked, tucking the quilt Mama gave me around my legs. Grandpap's truck didn't have a heater.

"A while yet."

"Are we halfway?"

"You ain't got the patience of a newborn gnat, Jane-Ery," Grandpap said. "You know what happened to the girl who married the bear?"

"Is this another of your stories?" I didn't much feel like listening to a story. Not when Richmond-city was so close!

"Just sit back," he said. "And I'll tell you about Whitebear Whittington.

"Long ever ago, there was a man with three daughters. He was going to town one day and he asked them what they wanted him to bring them."

"I heard this story already," I interrupted.

"No, you haven't. Now, hush." He went on. "The eldest daughter wanted a dress the color of all the birds in the sky. The second daughter asked for a dress of all the colors in the rainbow. But the youngest daughter wanted one white rose."

"The youngest daughters in these stories are dumb," I said.

Grandpap ignored me.

"The father went to town and got the dresses. On his way back home, he saw a bush loaded with white roses. As he broke one off, he heard a voice say, '*Give me what meets you first at the gate.*'

"The man had picked from a witch's rose bush and he had to pay. The man knew his old hound would meet him first, so he rode off, unworried.

"Instead of the hound, his youngest daughter met him at the gate. From the woods, the man heard the witch's voice, '*Send out my pay!*' He had no choice; he had to send out his youngest daughter. At the gate stood a big white bear. The girl climbed on the bear's back and went off with him.

"The bear lived in a fine house. He told the girl he was under a spell. During the day, he was a bear. At night, he was a man. He wanted her to be his wife, but she could never tell anyone his name, Whitebear Whittington, or he would go away forever. The girl promised.

"One day the girl's father came riding up," said Grandpap. "He wondered how she was gettin' along. He asked the name of her husband. The girl figured it wouldn't hurt to tell her father so she whispered, '*Whitebear Whittington.*'"

"Why do people in your stories always do what they shouldn't?" I asked.

"The girl's husband, who was a man at the time, heard and run off. She went after him in the woods. Everwhen she got lost, a white bird flew over and showed her the way. She met an old woman who needed help with her spinning and weaving. The girl helped her. The old woman gave her three gold nuts—a chinquapin, a hickory nut, and a walnut.

"'If ever you get in the trouble,' the woman told her, 'crack these nuts.'

"At last the girl found her husband, but he was sleeping like a bear in February. A witch had put a spell on him. The girl cracked the gold chinquapin first. Inside was gold wool. Next she cracked the gold hickory nut. A magic spinning wheel spun gold thread. Last she cracked the gold walnut. Out popped a loom that wove gold cloth.

"'I must have those,' said the witch. 'What'll you take for them?'

"'Break my husband's enchantment,' the girl said, 'and they will be yours.'

"Her husband woke up. He became a man all the time and they lived happy."

"That's a good story," I said. While I was listening, the sky had lightened enough so I could see out the window.

The crooked road had leveled out. Little white houses sat on neat square yards. Cows dozed in stubbly fields.

I peered at the passing landscape. "It's flat as a flittercake here."

Grandpap nodded. "These cows don't have two short legs like they do back home. Comes from grazing on a mountainside."

He turned onto a wide highway. Cars whizzed past at speeds that made my head swoony.

"Are we halfway *yet?*"

"Yep."

Halfway to Day's Bottom! My stomach felt fizzy from excitement.

I checked the paper bag tucked under my seat.

"I think we'll have good luck today," said Grandpap.

I hoped so. Grandpap wasn't the only one with plans.

the walnut man's granddaughter

The little white houses along the highway grew closer together. Soon we were in the city.

"Richmond!" I gawked at the statues marching down the street. Famous men like Robert E. Lee and George Washington sat straight-backed on huge horses. Electric lamps winked off as dawn ripened into day.

Grandpap parked his truck next to a man unloading pine wreaths. Pickups lined the wide street Grandpap said was the market. Men and women unloaded sacks and boxes from their truck beds.

"Who are all these people?" I asked Grandpap.

"Christmas peddlers," he replied. "They come from the hills—same as us—to sell greens and nuts."

People flocked around the peddlers, buying mistletoe shot from the tops of white oaks, running pine plucked from beneath forest leaves, holly branches heavy with red berries, roasting chestnuts, and Grandpap's walnuts.

"The Walnut Man!" A man wearing a soft tan coat and a checked scarf rushed over to shake Grandpap's hand. "Who is this you brought with you?"

"My granddaughter," Grandpap replied. "Jane-Ery helped me gather the nuts this year."

"Hello, Walnut Man's granddaughter," the man said. "Nice to meet you."

I mumbled hello, staring at his shoes. They were shiny and smooth, not cracked across the insteps like Grandpap's.

"How many this year?" Grandpap asked the man.

"Two. The missus always says, 'Frank, Christmas

isn't Christmas without black walnut cake.'"

It was my job to collect the money. While Grandpap was fetching the man's sacks, I slipped my paper sack from the truck cab. I pulled out my pine needle basket and held it out so the man could drop two dollars in it. Grandpap raised an eyebrow.

"Where did you get that basket?" the man asked me.

"Made it."

He ran his thumb around the neatly coiled rim. "My wife would love this. What will you take for it?"

"Whatever you think it's worth." I didn't look at Grandpap.

He dropped four quarters into my palm. "A dollar okay?"

A dollar! I'd never had that much cash-money before. I could buy Mama something pretty for Christmas. Maybe even have enough left over to buy Grandpap a new pair of shoes, fine shiny ones like the walnut-buying man's.

"I know what you're thinking," I said when we

were alone again. "I shouldn't sell my baskets. Grandpap, not everybody is like you."

"You're right about that," he said, clamping his teeth on his pipestem. He was fixing to say more, but then we got busy.

By noon we'd sold all our walnuts. We ate the dinner Mama packed, then walked down Broad Street. I clutched Grandpap's hand, afraid I'd get lost in the crowds.

Wonderment met my eyes at every turn. Store windows glittered with silver tinsel and gold stars. Why on earth would people want plain old pine decorations when they could gaze at such sights?

My heart beat faster. I had finally found Day's Bottom. Daddy was waiting for me. I didn't know where, but he'd see me, the way he'd spotted a bear's den across the valley.

"What are you going to do with that dollar?" Grandpap asked.

"Buy Mama a Christmas present."

I stopped in front of the tallest building I'd ever seen. *Thalheimers* was engraved over the golden doors. The fancy department store in Exie's newspaper. I wanted to refresh myself in the tearoom, like the ad said.

"Can we go in there?" I asked Grandpap.

He looked at a woman in a fur coat entering the golden door. "I think that store is a little out of your pocketbook range, Jane-Ery."

We walked a few more blocks. Streetcars let a bunch of people off, then started up again with a *clang-clang*. I wished I could ride on one.

"Why don't you do your shopping in here?" Grandpap said, pointing at a store with a plain front door. "I need to do a little business. I'll meet you on the sidewalk out front in an hour."

I didn't let on I wouldn't be there. No sense in over-worrying him.

G.C. Murphy's 5 & 10 was twice as big as Parson's. My feet pattered on the glossy black and white floor.

Cases and counters were heaped with things to buy.

I picked up a deep blue bottle of Evening in Paris and dabbed some on the inside of my wrist. It smelled like sugar-cake and Easter lilies.

Next I found a set of lace handkerchiefs, delicate as snowflakes, in a gold box tied with red ribbon. Mama didn't own anything so fine.

Then I wandered over to the candy counter. The candies displayed in fancy dishes were nothing like the penny-pick sweets at Parson's. Peppermint creams and rock candy gleamed behind the glass-front case like jewels. Chocolates and mints were stacked in tantalizing pyramids. My mouth watered.

The girl behind the counter smiled at me. She wore pale pink lipstick and a matching scarf in her hair. She smelled like the perfume I put on my wrist.

"May I help you?" she asked.

I looked at chocolate drops and butter mints and licorice whips. What would it hurt to buy myself candy? I had worked so hard picking walnuts and weaving baskets.

"I'll have some of those," I said.

"Half a pound of each?"

I nodded. That sounded about right.

She handed me three paper twists. I gave her one of my coins. She gave me back four pennies. I had spent almost a fourth of my basket money!

I decided to give Mama the candy as a treat. She'd had to stay home and feed the animals while Grandpap and I went gallivanting around the city.

In the shoe section, I found a pair of shiny brown shoes. They cost five dollars, a lot more than the seventy-nine cents I had left. I wouldn't be able to get Grandpap shoes after all.

Now I rushed through the store. I needed to find the perfect present for Mama. And then go meet Daddy. Not as a wavery notion this time, but for certain-sure.

And then I saw it.

A sparkly golden bracelet with a dangling heart. The heart opened so you could put tiny pictures inside. I held my breath as I peeked at the price tag.

Seventy-seven cents!

My palms sweated as I offered the last of my money to the jewelry counter girl. Would she think there was a mistake? Surely a bracelet that beautiful was worth a lot more.

But she wrapped the bracelet in cotton batting soft as lamb's wool, then laid it in a little silver box. She smiled as she handed it to me.

"Somebody's going to be surprised on Christmas morning," she said.

"My mother," I said.

"Well, she's a lucky lady to have such a thoughtful daughter."

I shoved the bracelet box in my coat pocket along with my two cents change.

Grandpap wasn't waiting outside. Good. I hated to worry him, but I had to find Daddy.

I wondered which part of Richmond was really Day's Bottom. Maybe way over yonder, where I could see a fancy church steeple.

As I walked, I pictured Daddy on the corner, or in front of that pretty church. Would he be wearing his red shirt? No, he'd have on city clothes—a navy silk tie, knife-creased pants.

The paper twists in my other coat pocket kept calling me. I dipped first into one, then another as I thought about more about Day's Bottom. All the ladies there were rich, like the ladies hurrying by me. The Day's Bottom ladies would clack along in high heels from Thalheimers and wear real diamonds.

Then I wondered if the heart bracelet fit me. I decided to try it on, just for a minute. Just to get the feel of wearing jewelry.

Mama didn't hold much with jewelry. She only wore the thin wedding band Daddy gave her on their wedding day. I could hear Mama on Christmas morning. She'd open the silver box and say, My, what a pretty thing, Jane-Ery. Then she'd put it in her bureau drawer. The heart bracelet shouldn't be locked away.

I took out the silver box. The heart sparkled in the bright sunshine. I shoved the box back in my pocket and wrapped the fine chain around my wrist. It kept sliding as my chocolate-sticky fingers fumbled with the clasp.

I saw it fall even before it did, like one of those dreams where you can't stop yourself from falling into a bottomless well. The golden bracelet slipped from my grasp like rainwater and slithered into a grate set in the sidewalk. I was left holding cold December air.

"No!" I fell to my knees and pressed my cheek against the iron bars. At first I couldn't see anything. As my eyes adjusted to the dimness, I strained to catch a glimpse of gold. But I couldn't pick out a curve of the heart or glint of the chain in the jumble of wet leaves and cigarette butts and chewing gum wrappers.

Mama's Christmas present was gone.

I started to cry.

Where was Daddy? Where was Grandpap? I didn't know how to get back to the five-and-dime store. The city was a mess of buildings and cars and streets. None of it made sense. Back home, I could find my way down Purgatory Mountain blindfolded by following rabbit trails and deer tracks.

People pushed by me with their packages, heads down, hats pulled low, dead-set on rushing home. I stood there, tears dripping off my chin. Nobody asked me what was wrong. Nobody cared. They eddied around me like I was a rock in the creek.

Daddy wasn't waiting for me. Not in this hateful place. He'd never take to wearing a necktie and folks would just make fun of his patched red shirt. The choking traffic would hem him in. Daddy didn't belong in Richmond-city.

And neither did I.

Grandpap found me sobbing on the sidewalk.

"You ain't hurt, are you?" he asked. "What are you doing so far from the store?"

"I—" I almost told him I had come here to find Daddy. I started over. "I spent my money on candy and a bracelet!" I said. "I ate the candy and lost the bracelet!"

"Where'd you lose the bracelet?"

"Down there!" I pointed to the grate. "Can you get inside it?"

Grandpap shook his head sadly. "Only city workers can open it. It's Saturday. They won't be workin' today." He patted my arm. "I'm sorry, Jane-Ery. But we'd best be headin' home."

We left the city. I stared out the window and didn't speak. Nothing Grandpap could say would make me feel better.

The little white houses grew farther apart. The cows were back in their barns.

I felt as ragged as the stubbly fields and thought about the story Grandpap told on the way to the city. Maybe I shouldn't have sold my basket. That cash-money gave me the big head. Greed jinxed my trip.

I wouldn't have been a bit surprised to hear the witch's voice say, *Send out my pay.*

the swan's gift

The mountains drained light from the day as we drove up into the foothills and chugged through the gap. A faint fingernail paring of a new moon rose above black treetops.

"Make a wish, Jane-Ery."

No moon-wish could fix my foolishness. Anyway, I'd had enough of his superstitions.

"Not in the mood," I said.

"Don't ever throw away a wish," Grandpap said. "It might could come true."

What should I wish for? To go back in time to just

before I dropped the bracelet down the grate?

What I really wanted was to go back in time before Daddy died. Maybe I could stop him from catching his ride that morning. Or make him linger over his dinner, so he wouldn't be in the path of that logging truck.

Now I was as foolish as Grandpap.

"Come on," he said.

With a sigh, I looked over my left shoulder and wished.

Suddenly he pulled the truck over on the shoulder of the road and switched off the engine. "Hear that?"

I didn't hear anything. "What?"

"Listen!"

I still couldn't hear anything. Then I heard faint cries high in the sky.

Woo-hoo. Woo-hoo.

The cries mingled with a rush of wingbeats, like a host of angels.

I held my breath and stared through the windshield.

Flying arrow-straight, long-necked birds crossed the moon-sliver by the hundreds.

"Are they geese?" I asked.

"Swans," Grandpap said. "I bet they were eating grain in them fields. See how the little birds fly behind the bigger ones? Protected-like."

The ribbon of swans spooled over stark woods, prettier than all the silver tinsel and glittery baubles in Richmond-city. The sight filled my sorrowed heart with joy, bottom to top.

I wondered how the birds could fly without running into each other. Then I noticed some swans shifted, letting other birds fly beside them, or go on ahead. There was order to their flight, like a school of minnows swimming in creek shallows.

We watched until the last swan disappeared over the ridge. The day had perished.

"Let's go home," I said to Grandpap. "Mama's probably wondering what happened to us."

"Wait a minute."

He got out of the truck and walked down the dark road. When he came back, he laid something soft and light in my palm.

A swan's feather.

"My Cherokee grandmother believed swan feathers have magical powers," he said. "If you keep this, you'll have swan medicine your whole life."

"How could you find a feather in the dark?" I asked.

He smiled. "Easy. It was in Day's Bottom."

I aimed to end this Day's Bottom business once and for all. Day's Bottom did not exist, any more than I'd seen Daddy those times.

"I thought Day's Bottom was far off yonder," I said, trying to catch him in a lie-tale.

"It can be as close as an eye-wink," he said.

Did he really think I believed him anymore? I leaned my head against the hard, cold window glass and did not say a word the whole way back home.

I knew right off what to do with the swan's feather. But I didn't know if I was good enough.

With a lapful of pine needles, I sat alone in the bedroom one night while Mama was baking. My only light came from a pine knot burning in a saucer on the side table.

I repeated Grandpap's words. "Weave without thinking about it. Get it in your hands."

After I began the first coil, I closed my eyes. Then I jabbed myself with the needle. Grandpap didn't mean weave *blind*, I told myself. He meant weave naturally, like flowers blooming in the spring, like rain washing a hot summer day clean and cool.

Like swans sailing against a crisp winter moon.

I thought about Daddy. How his face split in a grin when I ran outside to meet him after work. How he buttered my corncakes and saved the crispy rind of his side meat for me. How he swung me off the ground even after I got too big to pick up.

Then I thought about Mama. How she washed clothes with her battling stick and scoured the floor on her hands and knees. How she'd worked all day but was baking molasses cookies for Exie Dills because he'd helped us this fall.

The pine knot sputtered. Almost out.

I looked down. My hands cradled a tiny basket, about two inches across and perfectly round.

I took the swan's feather from under the mattress tick where I'd hidden it and wove its shaft into the rim. It became part of the pattern, stitches of white mingling with the rich brown pine needles. Since Daddy had died, I hadn't been sure of anything much, but this basket, I thought, was just right.

After tying off the last thread, I stroked the plumy crown. Was it my imagination, or did something touch the back of my hand, soft as my daddy's eyelashes when they brushed across my cheek?

Angel fingers.

falling weather

On Christmas Eve, Grandpap said, "You goin' to put your soup plate on the table for Santy?"

"Grandpap, I'm almost twelve. I don't believe in Santa Claus anymore."

He widened his eyes. "You don't! I do."

"But you're—" I pressed my lips together.

"'Old,'" he finished for me. "Well, I don't need a walking cane yet. And I still have dreams."

I wondered if I had any dreams left. I felt like the witch in the first story Grandpap told me. The one who had her moneypurse stolen by the hired girl. I'd been robbed of the biggest dream of all. Maybe it was time to put foolish notions behind me.

Mama came in from the porch, her wash-basket filled with cold-starched clothes off the line.

"Smoke's goin' to the ground," she said.

"Fallin' weather," Grandpap predicted. "I like a white Christmas." He handed me a rope of cranberries.

I climbed on a chair to loop the string around the top of the cedar Grandpap cut from our woods. He'd nailed a platform to the bottom of the trunk and set the tree in the corner well away from the stove.

Mama started fixing supper. On Christmas Eve, we always had oyster stew and stack cake drowned in cane syrup. Daddy and I used to see who could eat the most stack cakes. Last year—

I stopped. Time to put memories behind me too.

Grandpap helped me finish decorating the tree with paper chains, tinfoil stars, and gilded walnuts that Granny had made years ago.

"Come put your feet under the board," Mama said when supper was ready.

I didn't like oyster stew so Mama had made me succotash from the lima beans and corn she put up last summer. When I tasted the first milky spoonful, I was glad of the hours I'd hulled limas. Her stack cake was so good, I ate two big pieces.

After supper, Grandpap and I went outside to draw our night water from the pump. Like Mama said, smoke from the stovepipe streamed to the ground instead of curling up into the sky.

"Look yonder," said Grandpap.

The moon was new again, circled by a hazy ring. Ripply clouds crowded in from the west.

"Snow, for sure," he said. "My bones are chilled. We'd best get back in."

"I'll come in a minute."

"Take this, then." Grandpap threw his old coat around my shoulders.

I stood in the square of light from our front window and breathed in clean cold air. The air smelled like special, like a night a baby could be born in a far-off stable.

I looked up. Stars spread across the sky like a bed-quilt spangled with rhinestones. The brightest winked and shimmered above the lip of the Big Dipper. Daddy told me that was the North Star, the one that leads to true north. Was that the same star the Wise Men followed? I liked to believe it was.

Hugging Grandpap's coat around me, I went back inside the house.

Mama, Grandpap, and I sat in the glow of stove-light, adding a log now and then, talking about Christmases past, back when Mama was still a girl at home. Then Grandpap's chin drooped to his chest and Mama said it was time for bed.

Before I followed her into our room, I took a soup plate from the cupboard and set it at my place on the table.

I heard the snow first, a faint *scritch-scritch* against the windowpane. Daddy always said my hearing was so keen I could hear a field mouse walking on cotton.

Mama's side of the bed was empty. Used to be, I was always the first one up on Christmas morning. I'd run in here and jump on the bed between Mama and Daddy. Then I'd fly into the kitchen and see what goodies Santa Claus had left in my soup plate. Usually an orange and a banana, a sack of penny candy, sometimes a little doll or a rubber ball or a tin whistle.

I crawled under the bed and took out the basket I had wrapped in brown paper and tied with twine. Then I yanked my nightgown over my head and got dressed in a hurry. Heat from the woodstove didn't reach into our bedroom.

Grandpap was on the porch. Mama didn't see me hide her present under the tree.

All six eyes on the stove were busy with sizzling pans and steaming pots. Christmas breakfast was our big meal of the day. I smelled hominy grits, side meat, eggs, more oyster stew, coffee, fried potatoes, and cream gravy.

"Mornin'," Mama said. Her best apron was white with flour. "Take a turn beating these biscuits."

"Three hundred times?" I asked.

"Five," Mama said. "In honor of the day."

Even though my arm felt like it was going to break off, Mama's beaten biscuits were worth it. She only made them once or twice a year.

Grandpap came inside with an armload of kindling. He stamped snow from his boots and tossed the kindling into the wood basket.

"'Bout ready to eat?" he asked.

"When the biscuits are done," Mama told him.

I noticed my soup plate was gone. In its place Mama had put my regular plate. I guess it was silly of me to believe in Santa Claus.

I set jars of Mama's relish, blackberry preserves, apple butter, and a pitcher of buttermilk on the table.

When Mama pulled the biscuits from the oven, we sat down.

As Grandpap picked up the platter of side meat, Mama said, "I'd like Jane-Ery to give the blessing. After all, it is Christmas."

"Oh." Grandpap put the platter down, looking a little uncomfortable.

No one had said grace at a meal since Daddy died. But the three of us bowed our heads.

I thought a moment, then began, "Dear Lord, we thank thee for this beautiful day. And—" I swallowed. "We thank thee—" I was trying to add our family, but I choked.

Grandpap saved me. "And we thank thee for the vittles in front of us, near yet far. Amen." He picked up the platter again. "Let's eat!"

"Pap!" But Mama laughed.

After breakfast, I stacked the dishes on the drainboard.

"Let those go for now," Mama said. "Let's open our

gifts."

"Me first." I pulled out the lumpy paper-wrapped parcel and handed it to Mama with sweaty palms. I hoped she liked it but, what if she didn't? Next to any of Grandpap's baskets, mine was kind of clumsy.

Mama took forever and a day to untie the twine and slip off the paper. "I don't want to tear it," she said. "No sense wastin' good paper."

At last she held up the feather-crowned basket. Was it as pretty as I thought when I wrapped it? One side seemed a little crooked.

"Oh, my," she said after a few seconds. "Jane-Ery, did you make this?"

"Yes, I did. And without Grandpap's help."

"That's a fine basket," Grandpap said. "Looks like you got weavin' borned in you, Jane-Ery."

My heart beat faster. Why didn't Mama make over me? Why didn't she tell me it was the best gift she'd ever got?

"Do you like it?" I asked. My face felt hot, like I

was sitting too close to the stove.

Mama smiled. "Course I like it. You wove it your own self. It's beautiful." She set the basket on the table, next to Granny's blue and white sugar bowl. It looked homemade and dowdy, a poor excuse for a present.

"No, it's not," I blurted. "It's not as pretty as the bracelet I bought you in Richmond-city!"

"What bracelet?" Mama's eyebrows arched and she glanced at Grandpap. He busily tamped his pipe.

"I sold one of my baskets so I could buy you a Christmas present at G.C. Murphy's," I said. My words tumbling over each other, I told her how I ate the candy and lost the bracelet down a sidewalk grate.

Then I burst into tears.

"Now, don't carry on," Mama said. "I'd a hundred times druther have something you made than any store-bought present."

"No, you wouldn't," I said, sobbing.

"Jane-Ery, what has got into you?"

"I can't do anything to please you!"

"I said I love the basket. There is no cause for all this commotion."

I swiped my nose with the back of my hand. "I wanted to get you a special Christmas present. Not a dumb old basket!"

Mama stared at me. "What has brought all this on? I've never heard you carry on so—"

I couldn't stop crying. "All you do is work and tell me to do my chores!"

Mama took my hands in hers. Then she said, "Come along with me, Jane-Ery."

finding day's bottom

Mama led me into our bedroom. At the foot of the bed stood the blanket chest brought by her great-grandfather who came over from Germany back in the seventeen hundreds. Blue and red painted love-birds held a red painted heart between them in their beaks.

Mama lifted the lid and pulled out quilts and coverlets.

"What are you looking for?" I asked.

"You'll see."

At the very bottom of the chest was a bundle

wrapped in muslin. Mama spread out the bundle on the bed. I saw a pair of tiny pink booties, an envelope, and a small blanket.

"What's all this stuff?" I asked.

"Your things."

I stuck the booties on my fingers and walked them across my leg. "Did you knit these?" The wool was as fine as anything pulled from the gold chinquapin in Grandpap's story.

She nodded. "While I was waiting for you." She opened the envelope and showed me a ringlet of silky blonde hair tied with a faded blue ribbon.

"Your baby curl," she said. "From the first time I cut it. Look, it's the color of sourwood honey. Now your hair is a lot darker, like mine."

I touched the curl. It could have been spun from the magic spinning wheel that sprang from the golden hickory nut.

"We both cried when I cut your hair," Mama said. "You bawled because the scissors scared you. I cried because I didn't want my baby to grow up."

She smoothed the coverlet woven in shades of plum and moss green. "I wove this on my mother's old loom when I was in my eighth month. The clacking shuttle calmed you inside me."

I fingered the fringe. Not even the magic loom in the golden walnut could have made a finer coverlet.

"I've been so choice of it," Mama said, "never got it near water. I hung it over your cradle, so you could enjoy the colors."

I didn't understand. "Why are you showing me these things now?"

"Because I want you to see I already have the most special things in the world. You can't buy these at G.C. Murphy's or Parson's or anywhere." She patted my arm. "I can't buy you in a store, neither. Yes, you frazzle my nerves sometimes, 'specially this past year. But, Jane-Ery, you are my daughter. You're part of me, part of your daddy."

I looked at our reflection in the speckled mirror

over the dresser. I had my daddy's stick-straight hair, but it was the same color as Mama's, like she said. Funny. People always told me I took after my father. But now I saw Mama and I had the same stubborn chins. Maybe that was why we butted heads so much.

We went back in where Grandpap was waiting.

"Come see what Santy left in your soup plate," he said.

"He didn't leave anything in my soup plate," I said. "It was gone off the table this morning."

"Maybe he moved it. Santy can have secrets, too, you know."

The soup plate was now mysteriously under the tree. A small flat package wrapped in brown paper lay inside.

"What is it?" I asked.

"Open it and see," said Grandpap.

I slit the paper and pulled out a dark blue book. *People's National Bank* was stamped on the cover. Inside were dates and columns of numbers.

"It's a bank book," Mama explained. "A savings account. The money in there is your'n."

"Mine? But how can I have any money when—"

"We're broker than four 'clock?" The corners of Grandpap's mouth twitched. "Your daddy put that money away for you. For you to go to college."

I did not move. A present from Daddy! I never expected anything from him, ever again.

For a breath-catching second I thought he'd never been kilt in that accident, that he'd been at Day's Bottom all this time, that he was outside on the porch, waiting to come inside. He would stamp the snow off his boots, open the door and say, "Merry Christmas, Miss Mousie!" Then he'd spin me around even though I was too big.

I knew he'd never walk through the door. He was gone, as if I'd said his name out loud and did not know how to break the enchantment.

My mind rambled back to the day Daddy showed me the bear's den. All this spring and summer and fall it seemed I'd looked at everything front-ways. My eyes felt like I'd been staring straight into the fireball of the noonday sun. If only I would learn to look side-like, I might see things I didn't before, like the gap in the rock across the valley. And maybe it wouldn't hurt so much.

"Your daddy always told me he wanted you to have better," Mama said. "So he started scratchin' and scrimpin' for your college education."

"But . . . what about the tax bill?" I asked.

"Who told you about that?" Mama shot Grandpap a look. "Grandpap paid the back taxes. With the walnut money."

"Don't worry, Jane-Ery," he said. "We won't never touch your college money. And I'll lay back a few pennies when I can."

I began to cry again, noisy gulping sobs. Mama took me in her arms and rocked me like a baby.

"I know," she kept saying. "I know."

And I believe she did.

Grandpap gave me his big blue bandanna. "Great Scot! Is this any way to celebrate Christmas? Blow your nose, child."

Mama fetched the basket I made her and set it on the windowsill. "There's not another like it in the world."

I remembered the rows and rows of look-alike blue perfume bottles in G.C. Murphy's. I didn't feel so bad about not buying Mama a store-bought present. Everybody in Richmond-city must smell the same.

That evening after supper, Grandpap declared, "We need some air to get the stink blowed off."

Laughing and talking, we all buttoned up our coats and stomped into boots.

It had stopped snowing. Snow capped the milk pails, soft as swan's feathers, light as my mother's beaten biscuits. The new moon glittered in the dark blue sky.

I knew then we were all in exactly the right place—the bottom of the day.

"Well," Grandpap said. "Folks hanker all year for Christmas and now Christmas is as far away as it ever was."

"Pap," Mama said. "You and your fool-talk."

He pointed. "Jane-Ery, see that rabbit a'stirrin' under that bush? That means snow again tomorrow."

Daddy had a saying, "If we all touch hands, we can get this done." That was his way of tackling big jobs.

I reached over and touched Grandpap's hand. Then I curled my other hand in my mother's. Though it was cold outside, our hands were warm.

Tree boughs clattered in a gust of wind. I'd never paid attention to the clutter of branches that seemed to grow every which way. Now I could see limbs outlined against the indigo sky, each twig part of the pattern, each stem on this earth for a reason.

This time I heard them first. *Woo-hoo, woo-hoo.*

They came by the hundreds, necks outstretched, flying straight as a ribbon across the moon.

One big, strong swan led the way with powerful

wingbeats. A smaller swan followed right along behind, protected-like.

acknowledgments

Once when I was speaking at a small school in the Virginia mountains, a woman stepped forward with a gift. Inside the bag was a tiny bird's nest of a basket, its base a polished walnut slice. The woman said the pine-needle basket had been made by an elderly man whose Cherokee grandmother taught him the craft. I marveled at the basket's perfection and promised to weave it into a story someday.

Seasons passed. The basket sat in my office, a reminder of my promise. Outside, birds built nests in the pear tree, raised families, left again. The leaves fell, revealing wondrous creations of grass and sticks and Christmas ribbons, woven with skillful beaks and tiny feet.

Twice a year, I flew to Vermont for writing classes. The pine-needle basket story trailed behind me. My wise adviser, Jane Resh Thomas, knew this book was ready to hatch. When I insisted it was not a novel, but a collection of linked episodes, she let me back into the book. When it was born, she carried the pieces of my protests away, protecting my story, which was whole and sweet, but still very new.

I hovered over the book anxiously, hesitant to send it to my editor, Shannon Barefield. I need not have worried. Shannon gently prodded it to the edge of the nest, nudging me with just the right questions and suggestions, and helped it fledge. Together, we have made this book the best it can be.

I leaned on Richard Chase's *Grandfather Tales* as the basis for Grandpap's stories. Chase traveled the Appalachian mountains of Virginia and North

Carolina in the 1940s, collecting and writing down the old stories people told him.

I would like to thank my husband, Frank, for his support over the years and for his unwavering belief in this book. Lastly, I wish to thank those closest to me who have flown ahead.

about the author

Candice Ransom grew up in shadow of the Blue Ridge Mountains of Virginia, where Jane-Ery's story takes place. Ms. Ransom's passion for the people and stories of the South has shaped many of her one hundred books for children. Her fiction and picture books have been named to the New York Public Library's 100 Best Children's Books list, the ABA *Bookselling This Week* Kids' Pick of the Lists, and the Virginia Young Readers' List. She lives in Fredericksburg, Virginia.